9/22

5-

Nora Jane and Company

Nora Jane and Company

Ellen Gilchrist

BLOOMSBURY

First published as *The Courts of Love* in the United States of America 1996

First published in Great Britain 1997
Bloomsbury Publishing Plc, 38 Soho Square, London W1V 5DF

Copyright © 1996 by Ellen Gilchrist

A CIP catalogue record for this book is available from the British Library

ISBN 0 7475 3335 0

10 9 8 7 6 5 4 3 2 1

Printed in Great Britain by Clays Ltd, St Ives plc

"... for the lovers, their arms
Round the griefs of the ages,
Who pay no praise or wages
Nor heed my craft or art."

—Dylan Thomas

And for Mike Mattil, friend and counselor, purveyor of commas and common sense, font of knowledge.

"Just remember when you're feeling very small and insecure, how amazingly unlikely is your birth. And pray that there's intelligent life somewhere up in space, cause there's bugger all down here on earth."

—Monty Python

"To hell with elitist fashion; to hell with elitist guilt; to hell with existentialist nausea; and above all, to hell with the imagined that does not say, not only in, but behind the images, the real."

—John Fowles

Contents

Nora Jane
and Company

IN WHICH THE FATHERS of the twin girls Tammili and
Lydia Whittington meet again. One would think this was
inevitable. Their DNA had swum together for nine
months, hands touching, legs embracing. In many ways
they are closer than either of them are to the mother.
These three people, caught forever in Indra's net. The net
of jewels, in which each jewel contains the reflections of
all the others. The twins are ten years old. Freddy Harwood is forty-four. Sandy George Wade is thirty-one.
Nora Jane is twenty-nine. The universe is several trillion
million and beginning to coalesce. Nineteen ninety-five
and we are still in orbit. Keep your fingers crossed.

Perhaps a Miracle

IT WAS THE WORST argument they had had in months. Nora Jane almost never argued with Freddy Harwood. In the first place she thought he was smarter than she was and in the second place he always went rational on her and in the third place there were better ways to get what she wanted. The best way was to say she wanted something and then not mention it for a week or two. All that time he would be arguing with himself about his objection and in the end he would decide he didn't have the right to impose his ideas on any other human being, not even his wife. Freddy had not gone to Berkeley in the sixties for nothing. *The Greening of America* and *The Sorcerer of Bolinas Reef* were still among his favorite books. Once a reporter had asked Freddy to name his ten favorite books and he had left out both those books because this was the nineties and Freddy was famous in the world of publishing and independent bookstores and he didn't want to seem too crazy in public. If someone had asked him the ten things he regretted most, leaving *The Greening of America* and *The Sorcerer of Bolinas Reef* off his list would have been right up there with the butterfly tattoo on his ankle.

"It doesn't matter what you take," he said out loud. "It's none of my business."

"You don't care what I take?"

"All I said is that sociology is a pseudoscience and you're too good for that kind of mush. I didn't mean you shouldn't take it. I should never have asked what you are going to take. I'm embarrassed that I asked. All I care about is that you be home by three so the girls won't come home to an empty house."

"You don't want me to go to college. I can tell."

"I want you to go to college fiercely. I wish I could quit work and go with you. My biology is about twenty years behind the field."

"Freddy." She climbed down off the ladder. She had been putting up drapes while Freddy read. She was wearing a white cashmere sweater and a pair of jeans. She was wearing ballet shoes.

"You wear that stuff to drive me crazy," Freddy said. "If they sold that perfume Cleopatra used on Caesar, you'd wear it every day. How can I let you go to college? Every man at Berkeley will fall in love with you. Education will come to a grinding halt. No one will learn a thing. No one will be able to teach. It's my civic duty to keep you at home. I owe it to the culture." He pulled her across the room and began to dance with her. He sang an old Cole Porter song in a falsetto voice and danced her around the sofas. One thing about Nora Jane. She could move into a scenario. "Where are the girls?" she asked.

"In the den doing homework. I told them I'd take them down to Berkeley to get an ice cream cone when they were finished."

"Meet me in the pool house. Hurry." She smiled the wild, hard-won smile that worked on Freddy Harwood better than all the perfumes of the East.

"Yes, yes, yes," he answered, and let her go and she walked away from him and out of the room and down the stairs and across the patio to the guest house beside the swimming pool. She went into the bedroom and took off her clothes and waited. In a moment he was there. He turned off the lights to the pool with a switch on the wall. He locked the door and lay down beside her and began to make love to her.

It was Freddy's theory that the way you made love to a woman was to worship every inch of her body with your heart and mind and soul. This was easy with Nora Jane. He had worshiped every inch of Nora Jane since the night he met her. He loved beauty, had been raised to know and worship beauty, believed beauty was truth, balance, order. He worshiped Nora Jane and he loved her. Ten years before, on a snow-covered night in the northern California hills, he had delivered the twin baby girls who were his daughters. With no knowledge of how to do it and nothing to guide him but love, he had kept them all alive until help came. Nora Jane had another lover at the time and no one knew whose sperm had created Lydia and Tammili. Most of the time Freddy Harwood didn't give a damn if they were his or not. They lived in his home and carried his name and gave his life meaning and kept Nora Jane by his side. The other man had disappeared before they were born and had not been heard from since. It was a shadow, but all men have shadows, Freddy knew. Where it was darkest and there was no path. This was Freddy's credo. Each knight entered the forest where it was darkest and there was no path. If there was a path, it was someone else's path.

Freddy ran his hand up and down the side of Nora Jane's body. He trembled as he touched her small round hip. I cultivate this, he decided. Well, some men gamble.

II

A FOUR-YEAR-OLD boy named Zandia, who was visiting his grandmother in the house next door, had been trying all week to get to the Harwoods' heated swimming pool. He didn't necessarily want to get in the water. He wanted to get the blue and white safety ring he could see from his grandmother's fence. All these days and his grandmother had not noticed his fascination with the pool. Perhaps she had noticed it but she hadn't given it enough weight. She trusted the lock on the gate, and besides, Zandia was such a wild little boy. He could have four or five plans of action going at the same time. His latest fascination was with vampires, and Clyda Wax, for that was his grandmother's name, had been occupied with overcoming his belief in them. "Where did you ever see a vampire?" she kept asking. "There is no such thing as a vampire, Zandia. There are vampire bats. I'll admit that. But they live in caves and they are very stupid and blind and I could kill a hundred of them with a broom."

"They would fly up and eat your blood. They can fly."

"I'd knock them down with the broom. They are blind. It would be easy as pie. I'd have a bushel basket full of them."

"They'd fly up and stick to the trees. What would you do then?"

"I'd get a giraffe to eat them."

"But giraffes live in Africa."

"So what? I can afford to import one."

"What about Count Dracula? You couldn't kill him."

"There isn't any Count Dracula. There's just that vulgar, disgusting, imbecilic Hollywood trash that you are exposed to in L.A. I shudder to think what they let you watch down there. Did the baby-sitter show it to you? Did the baby-sitter tell you about vampires? Vampires are not true. Now go and play with your Jeep for a while. I want to rest." Clyda closed her eyes and lay back on the lawn chair. She didn't mean to go to sleep but she was exhausted from taking care of him. She had volunteered for one week. It had turned into three. He had been up that morning at five rummaging around in her kitchen drawers. "When your mother comes to get you I'm going to a spa," she said sleepily. "I'm going to Maine Chance and stay a month."

As soon as he saw she was asleep he walked over to the fence and undid the latch. He pushed the latch open and disappeared through the gate. There it was, shimmering in the moonlight, the swimming pool with all its chairs and the red rubber raft and the safety ring. He walked under the window of the bedroom where Nora Jane and Freddy lay in each other's arms. He walked around the chairs and up to the edge of the water. He bent over and saw his reflection in the water. Then he began to fall.

"Something's wrong." Nora Jane sat up. She pushed Freddy away from her. She jumped up from the bed. She tore open the door and began to run. She got to the pool just as Zandia was going under. She ran around the edge. She jumped in beside him and found him and they began to struggle. She pulled and dragged him through the water. When she got to the shallow end she pulled him up into the air. Then the lights were on and Freddy was in the water with her and they lifted him from the water and turned him upside down and Freddy was on the mobile phone calling 911.

"How did you know?" they asked her. After it was over and Zandia was in his grandmother's arms eating cookies and the living room was full of uniformed men and Tammili and Lydia had seen their naked parents performing a miracle and were the most cowed ten-year-old girls in the Bay Area.

"I don't know. I don't know what I knew. I just knew to go to the pool."

"You've never even met this kid?" one of the men in uniform asked.

"I've seen him in the yard. He's been in the yard next door."

Later that night, after Zandia and his grandmother had been walked to their house and Tammili had been put to bed reading *The Voyage of the Dawn Treader* and Lydia had been put to bed reading a catalog from *American Girl* and they were alone in their room, Freddy had opened all the windows and the skylight above the bed and they had lain in each other's arms, awed and pajamaed, talking of time and space and life at the level of microbiology and wave and particle theory and why Abraham Pais was their favorite person in New York City and how it was time to take the girls to the Sierra Nevada to see the mountains covered with snow. "We need to do something to mark it. Plant some trees at Willits. Lay bricks for a path."

"You could rearrange the books in the den. It's such a mess in there Betty won't even go in to clean. It's unhealthy to have that many books in a room. It's musty. It's like a throwback to some other age. It doesn't go with the rest of the house."

"Go on to sleep if you can."

"I can. You're the one who doesn't sleep."

"We should both sleep tonight. Something's on our side. I never felt that as strongly as I do right now." He patted her for a while. Then he began to dream his old dream of building the house at Willits. The solar house he and Nieman had built by hand to prove it could be done and to prove who they were. Our rite of passage into manhood house, Freddy knew. The house to free us from our mothers. In the recurrent dream it was a clear, cold day. They had finished the foundation and were beginning to set the posts at the sides. The mountain lions came and sat upon the rise and watched them. "You think I'm nuts to go to all this trouble to make a nest," he told the lions. "Well, you're wrong. This is what my species does."

In that magical house Tammili and Lydia were born and sometimes Freddy thought the house had been built to serve that purpose. To make them so much his that nothing could sever the bond. So what if one or both of them were Sandy George Wade's biological spawn? So what if maybe Tammili was his and Lydia was not? So what in a finite world if there was love? Freddy always ended up deciding.

Next door, it was Zandia's grandmother who couldn't sleep. She was talking to Zandia's mother on the phone. "You just come up here tomorrow afternoon as soon as they finish shooting and spend the night. He's lonely for you. Four-year-old boys shouldn't be away from their mother for this many days."

"I can't. We have to look at rushes every night. It's the first time Sandy and I have had a chance to be in a film together. I'm a professional, Mother. I have to finish my work, then I'll come get him. There's no reason you can't hire a baby-sitter for him, you know. He stays with baby-sitters here."

"He almost died, Claudine. I don't think you understand what happened here. You never listen to me, do you know that? You only half listen to anything I say. The child almost died. Also, he is obsessed with vampires. Who let him see a movie about vampires? That's what I'd like to know. I'm taking him to my psychiatrist tomorrow for an evaluation."

"All right then. I'll send someone to get him. I thought you wanted him, Mother. You always do this. You say you want him, then you change your mind in about four days."

"He almost drowned."

"Could we talk in the morning? I'll call you at seven."

Claudine hung up the phone, then went into the bedroom to find Sandy. He was in bed smoking and reading the script. He put the cigarette out when he saw her and shook his head. "Where have you been?" he asked. "What took you so long?"

"Zandia fell in a swimming pool and Mother's neighbor had to fish him out. They're acting like it was some sort of big, big deal. God, she drives me crazy. This is the last time he's going up there. From now on if she wants to see him she can come down here."

"We'll be finished in a week or ten days. It can't drag on much longer than that. You think we ought to send for him?"

"She can bring him. I'll tell her in the morning. I'll line up a sitter and he can go back to the Montessori school in the mornings. I knew better than to do this."

"How'd he fall in a pool?"

"Mother's neighbors left the gate open or something. The police came. He's fine. Nothing happened to him. It's just Mother's insanity."

Then Sandy George Wade, who was the father of Lydia Harwood, as anyone who looked at them would immediately know, began to flip channels on the television set, hoping to find a commercial starring either Claudine or himself, as that always cheered him up and made him think he wouldn't end up in a poor folks home. He reached for Claudine, to believe she was there, and sighed deep inside his scarred, motherless, fatherless heart. His main desire was to get a good night's sleep so he would be beautiful for the cameras in the morning.

Claudine pulled away from him. She got up and went into the other room to call her mother back. When she returned she had a different plan. "We have to go to San Francisco and pick him up. She won't bring him. Well, to hell with it. She wants me to meet the woman who pulled him out of the pool. I probably ought to sue them for having an attractive nuisance. Anyway, we have to go. Will you take me?"

"Of course I will. As soon as we have a break. Come on, get in bed. I like San Francisco. It's a nice drive. We'll take the BMW. It's driving good since I got the new tires. Get in bed. Let's get some sleep." Then Claudine gave up for the day and climbed into the bed and let Sandy cuddle up to her. Their neuroses fit like gloves. They were really very happy together. They hated the same things. They liked to make love to each other and they liked to sleep in the same bed. It was the best thing either of them had ever known. They even liked Zandia. Neither one of them liked to take care of him but they didn't hate or resent him. Sometimes they even thought he was funny.

Lunch at the Best Restaurant in the World

"So why was I chosen for this? That's what I keep asking myself. It's like a tear in the fabric of reality. Maybe I heard him walking by the window. I have a perfect ear for music. Well, I do. Maybe I saw him by the fence and knew he'd be wanting to get to the pool. All mothers are wary of pools. I've been watching to make sure no one drowns in our pool for years. Maybe there's a logical explanation. I'm sure there is. It only seems like a miracle." Nora Jane was talking. She and Freddy and Freddy's best friend, Nieman Gluuk, were at Chez Panisse having lunch. Nora Jane was wearing yellow. Freddy had on his plaid shirt and chinos. Nieman wore his suit. It was the first time the Harwoods had been out in public since the night Nora Jane pulled the child from the swimming pool. Nieman had been with them almost constantly since the event. Actually he had been with them almost constantly since they were married ten years before. Nieman and Freddy saw each other or talked on the phone nearly every day. They had done this since they were five years old. No one thought anything about it or ever said it was strange that two grown men were inseparable.

"Three knights were allowed to see the Grail," Freddy said. "Bors and Percival and Galahad. They were pure of heart. You're pure of heart, Nora Jane. And besides, you're an intuitive. The first time Nieman met you he told me that. He says you're the most intuitive person he's ever known."

"Maybe this means I shouldn't go to college. It means something, Freddy. Something big."

"You think I don't know that? I was there too, wasn't I? I watched it happen. What it means is that there's a lot more going on than we are able to acknowledge. Thought is energy. It creates fields. You picked up on one. You're a good receiver. That's what intuitive means. Maybe I'll go to school with you. Just dive right into a freshman science course and see if I sink or swim."

Nieman sighed and shook his head from side to side. "I can't believe you had this experience just when you were getting ready to try your wings at Berkeley. It's a coincidence, not a warning. It doesn't mean the girls are in danger or that we are in danger. No, listen to me. I know you think that but you shouldn't. The point is that you saved his life, not that his life was in danger. You will always save lives in many ways. It's all the more reason to go back to school and gain more knowledge and more power. Knowledge is power, even if it does sound trite to say it."

"I wish they hadn't put it in the papers." Nora Jane turned to Nieman and touched his hand. She was one of the three people in the world who dared to touch the esteemed and feared Nieman Gluuk, the bitter and hilarious movie critic of the *San Francisco Chronicle*. "The whole thing only lasted about six minutes. I can barely remember any of it except the moment I knew to do it. Freddy remembers pulling him out better than I do."

"We must never forget it," Nieman said.

"A man who had it happen to him last year called last night. He went through a glass door to get to a pool and saved his nephew. He thinks it has something to do with water. Water as a conductor."

"It proves a lot of theories," Freddy added. "I was there too, Nieman. I witnessed it. I was in bed with her."

"Excuse me." They were interrupted by a waiter, who took

their orders for goat cheese pie and salads and wine. "It was the single most profound thing that ever happened to me in my life," Freddy went on. "I will be thinking about it every day for the rest of my life. A tear in the cover, a glimpse of a wild, or perhaps exquisitely orderly, reality that is lost to us most of the time. Think of it, Nieman. The brain can't stand to consciously process all it senses and knows. We'd go crazy. The brain is a filter and its first job is to keep the body healthy. Occasionally, perhaps by accident, it sees a larger reality as its domain. Altruism. Well, it's so humbling to be part of it." He looked down, afraid they would think he wanted them to remember what he had done in the earthquake of 1986. But they knew better. He had forbidden his friends ever to speak of that. "Well, let's don't talk it all away. It's Nora Jane's miracle. I want to take her up to Willits for a while to think it over but she can't go. She starts school in three days, you know."

The waiter put bread down in front of them, the best French bread this side of New Orleans. Nieman held out a loaf to Nora Jane and they broke the bread. They ate in silence for a while.

"Fantastic about Berkeley," Nieman said at last. "Brilliant. I wish I could go. I feel like a dinosaur with my old knowledge. My encyclopedia is twenty years old. Every year I say I'll get another one but I never do."

The waiter brought more bread. Nieman buttered a piece and examined it, calculating the fat grams and wondering if it mattered. "Our darling Nora Jane," he went on. "Loose on the campus in the directionless nineties. I should write a modern opera for you. The problem is the ending. Shakespeare knew what to do. He poured in outrageous action, tied up all the loose ends, piled up some bodies, and danced off the stage on the wings of language. Ah, those epilogues. 'As you from crimes would pardoned be. Let your indulgence set me free.' Oh, he could lift the language! The modern stage can't bear the weight of so much beauty, so much fun. It's too large an insult to the modern fantasy, boredom, and self-pity. I went to three movies last week that were so bad I didn't last for the first hour. I just walked out. They began hopefully enough, were well acted by fine actors, then you could see the money mold begin to grow, the meetings where the money people in group think begin to decide how to corrupt the script. Well, let's not ruin lunch with such thoughts. After lunch shall we go over to the campus and walk around and get you accustomed to your new domain, Miss Nora? I heard the brilliant translator Mark Musa is here for the semester to teach *The Divine Comedy.* You might want to take that. We could go by and see if he's in his office and introduce ourselves."

"There you go," Freddy said. "Trying to take over what she takes. I pray to God every day to make me stop caring what classes she takes."

"The only answer is for you to go with me. You too, Nieman. Why not? Life is short, as you both tell me a thousand times a month."

"Life is short," Nieman agreed. "We could do it, Freddy. We could think of it as a donation to the university. Pay tuition as special students, sign up for classes, and go as often as we are able. I could take Monday and Tuesday off. I'm going to list the names of seven movies and then leave a blank white space. Think of us back on the campus, Freddy. Freddy was valedictorian of our class, Nora. But you know that."

"His mother's told me a million times. I think it was the high point of her life."

"That's what she wants you to think. The high point of her life was when she flew that jet to Seattle in the air show. No, I guess it was when she played Martha in *Who's Afraid of Virginia Woolf?* You know who she's going out with now, don't you, Nieman?"

"I heard. It's a terrible shadow, Freddy, but you have survived so far. Well, shall we do it then? Register for classes?"

"Yes. I'm taking biology, physics, and a history course. I want to see what they're teaching. It can't be as bad as I've heard it is."

"I'll take Musa's Dante in Translation and a playwriting course. I'll go incognito and write the play for Nora Jane and we'll put it on next year as an AIDS benefit."

"I'll sing 'Vissi d'arte' from the side of the stage while twelve little girls in long white dresses run around the stage doing leaps. Would that be a conclusion? Then a poet can run out on the stage and read part of 'Little Gidding.' Imagine us all going to college together."

"Meeting for coffee at Aranga's. When I was a student I was touched by old people going back to school. We will touch their silly little hearts. At least, Freddy and I will. You'll drive them crazy. I don't know, Freddy, maybe she's overeducated already."

"I want a degree. I'm embarrassed not to have a college degree. I'm the first person in my family in three generations not to have one." She sat up very straight and tall and Nieman and Freddy understood this was not to be taken lightly.

"Then let's go," Freddy said. "If you will allow us, we will accompany you on this pilgrimage." She turned her head to look at him and he fell madly in love with the sweep and whiteness of her neck and Nieman watched this approvingly. After all, someone has to be in love and get married and continue the human race.

An hour later they were on the Berkeley campus, walking along the sidewalks where Freddy and Nieman had walked when they were young. Nora Jane had been on the campus many times but never as a student. It was very strange, very liberating, and she felt her spirit open to the world she was about to enter. "I'll be Virgil and you be Dante and Nora Jane can be Beatrice," Nieman was saying. "The possibility of vast fields of awareness, that's what this campus always says to me. I used to think I could get vibrations from the physics building when the first reactor was installed and all those brilliant minds were here. I used to feel the force of them would dissolve the harm my mother did to me each morning. She would pour fear and anxiety over me and I would step onto the campus and feel it eaten up by knowledge. She was enraged that I was studying theater. She was very hard on me."

"You had to live at home with her?" Nora Jane took his arm to protect him from the past.

"She wanted me to go to medical school and be a psychiatrist, as she was seeing one. I would say to her, Mother, theater is psychotherapy writ large. The actors on the stage do what people do in ordinary life, keep secrets, say half of what they're thinking, manipulate, lie. Because it's writ large on the stage or screen the audience is on to them. They leave the theater and go out into the world more aware of other people's behaviors, if not of their own. Still, she was not convinced. She still thinks what I do is frivolous."

"She can't, after all these years?"

"Can she not? I'm an only child, don't forget that."

"I am too and so is Freddy. We're the only-child league. Like the red-headed league in Sherlock Holmes."

They linked arms, coming down the wide sidewalk to the student union. "This is like *The Wizard of Oz,*" Nieman said. "In *The Divine Comedy* they walked single file."

"Well, these are not the legions of the damned either," Freddy added, "although they certainly look the part." They were passing students, some with rings in their ears and noses and lips and some wearing chic outfits and some looking like they were only there because they didn't have anything better to do.

"Let's go to the registrar's office and get that over with," Freddy suggested.

"I will fill out any number of forms but I am not sending off for transcripts," Nieman decreed. "If they start any funny stuff about transcripts I'll drop my disguise and call the president of the university."

"We aren't pulling rank, Nieman," Freddy said. "We go as pilgrims or not at all."

"You go your way and I'll go mine, as always. Yes, it's beginning to feel like old times."

"Don't talk about the sixties or I'll hit you. I was in a convent school kneeling in the gravel before the statue of the Virgin and you were here getting to read literature and hear lectures by physicists. It isn't fair. You're too far ahead. I'll never catch up."

"No competition please. We're in this together."

By five that afternoon it was done. Freddy was signed up to audit World History and Physics I and Biology I. Nieman was taking Dante and had met Mark Musa and promised to brush up on his Italian and Nora Jane had her books and notebooks for

English, History, Algebra, and Introduction to Science. They had sacks of books from Freddy's bookstore and the campus bookstore.

When they were through collecting all the books they went to a coffeehouse across the street from the campus and picked out a table where they could meet. "I don't know if this table will be large enough," Nieman said. "Students will be flocking to us, don't you think?"

"Don't scare me like that," Freddy said.

"Don't turn my education into an anecdote," Nora Jane decreed. "Or I'll get my own table and have my own following." She piled her books up in front of her and looked at them. She was proud of them. She was on fire at this beginning.

The Incursions of the Goddamn Wretched Past

It was the Sunday morning after the wonderful Friday when Nora Jane, Freddy, and their best friend, Nieman, spent the afternoon on the Berkeley campus signing up for classes and being filled with happiness and hope.

It was Sunday morning and Freddy and Nora Jane were on the patio reading the Sunday newspapers and watching Zandia, who was brandishing a plastic sword in the air. He was standing on a ladder by the fence that separated the houses and pretending to poke them with the sword to punish them for ignoring him.

Because Nora Jane had saved Zandia's life he thought he had a claim on her. He thought she was a mean, bad girl to sit there reading the newspapers when he didn't have a thing to do. "I'm killing you," he called out in his annoying, high-pitched voice. "You are Nora Jane Captain Hook. I'm swording you."

"You think I should go get him?" Nora Jane asked Freddy. "Clyda said his mother was coming this afternoon. Can you stand him for a while?"

"Sure. Why not? Did that man call about the new pool cover?"

"He's coming Monday afternoon. Betty will let him in if I'm

not here." Nora Jane got up from her chair and walked down across the lawn to Zandia, who was continuing to threaten her. His grandmother met her at the fence.

"Let me take him for a while," Nora Jane asked. "We like to watch him play."

"If you're sure you want him. I swear to God I'm worn out with him. I'm going to Maine Chance for two weeks the minute that he's gone. I was going to the Golden Door but they're full."

"Let us have him for a while. It will keep Freddy from reading the editorial page. It drives him crazy to read the editorials. Actually he shouldn't even be allowed to read the papers." Nora Jane helped Zandia over the fence and he stood beside her, poking his sword in the direction of his grandmother.

"Claudine ought to be here by three or four. They sent me some stills from the set. You want to see them? She really is a pretty girl. I guess I'm too proud of her." Clyda pulled some photographs out of the pocket of her jacket. She handed them over the fence, still talking. "That's Kevin Kline in the background. That's a Mardi Gras parade. These were made while they were still filming in New Orleans. That's Claudine and the other one's her boyfriend, Sandy Wade. They're pretty handsome, aren't they?"

Nora Jane took the photographs. It was Sandy George Wade, her old lover. Ten years older and stronger looking and wider and twelve times as handsome, if it were possible for anyone that handsome to look any better. It was Sandy, on his way to San Francisco to ruin her life.

"That's her boyfriend?"

"Yes. He's very good-looking, isn't he? They'll be here this afternoon to get Zandia. Claudine wants to meet you and thank you in person. She'll never forgive me if she doesn't have a chance to thank you for what you did."

"I don't know if we'll still be here. We're going to Berkeley starting tomorrow. There's so much we have to do. Well, thanks for showing these to me." Nora Jane handed them back over the fence. "I'll bring him back in half an hour. We have to leave pretty soon." She took Zandia's hand and hurried back across the lawn to Freddy. Tammili and Lydia were with him. Tammili

had on a blue and white dress and Lydia had on shorts and a
white T-shirt advertising an Amos Oz book.

Lydia is his, Nora Jane said to herself. If he sees her he will
know. Anyone will know. We know. Freddy will go crazy when
he finds out Sandy's coming. Well, I can't wait. I have to tell him
now. We have to leave. What hell is this? That we have to pay
for the past forever. The terrible past. The mean past. It's here
every moment of our lives, weighing us down, ruining everything we do.

"Take Zandia," she said to Tammili. "Go find him some cookies. I have to talk to your father."

She pulled Freddy up from his chair and led him into the
living room. It was a perfect room. High glass walls that
looked out onto the bay. White marble floors with soft blue
handmade cotton rugs. A long gold sofa. A Japanese tea box
for a coffee table. A bowl of white roses beside the fireplace.
Nora Jane pushed a button and the music of Johann Se-
bastian Bach began to play. Freddy had not spoken. He thought
she was going to tell him someone had died. He was going
over a list in his head. It had to be something Zandia's grandmother told her. It wouldn't be Nieman, or someone would have
called.

"Sit down," she said. "Don't go crazy when you hear this. We
can deal with this. We are not hopeless in the face of what I'm
going to tell you."

"Say it."

"Sandy Wade is the boyfriend of Zandia's mother. They're
coming here today. This is real, Freddy. I just saw a photograph
of him. We can't let him see Lydia. He's a human being. It would
break his heart and then I don't know what he'd do. He's in a
film with Zandia's mother. Clyda has photographs of the girls
with Zandia at the pool. He'll see them. We can get the girls out
of here but what about the pictures? Even if we could do
something about that, Clyda will talk about them. He thinks
they're his. Both of them. I lived with him the whole time I was
pregnant. Don't forget that."

"We'll steal the photographs. That's easy. Say you want to borrow them." He had stood up. He was walking around the room.

"She gave us a set."

"I'm going to get them now. We'll sell the house. We'll move. I'll sell the house tomorrow."

"That's overreacting."

"No, it's not. Call Mother. Tell her we're coming over there for a few days. Then we'll go get the photographs. You keep her busy and I'll steal them."

Twenty minutes later Nora Jane and Freddy were in the kitchen of Clyda's house. "We want to see those photographs you took," Freddy said. "We need to borrow the negatives. We can't find the ones you gave us. The girls must have put them somewhere."

"Oh, they are good, aren't they? I can't believe how well they turned out." Clyda left the room to get the photographs. Zandia stuck his sword into the space between the refrigerator and the wall. The cat climbed up on a counter and sat beside a plate of fruit. The doorbell was ringing. Then the phone was ringing also. Nora Jane started to answer it, then couldn't touch it. Zandia picked up the phone. It was Lydia, looking for her mother. "Put my mother on the phone, Zandia. Zandia, can you hear me? Is my mother there?"

There were excited voices in the hall. Zandia dropped the phone and ran down the hall and then they were there. His mother and his grandmother and Sandy George Wade, moving into the kitchen all talking. Freddy had never met Sandy Wade but he had lived with Lydia for ten years and it was as though she had stepped into the room. The hair, the eyes, the body English, the expression on Sandy's face, quizzical, waiting.

"I have wondered where you were," Nora Jane began. "I'm glad to see you well. This is my husband, Freddy. Sandy is an old friend from New Orleans," she explained to Clyda. "We went to school together."

"We went to the same church," Sandy added. "We knew each other a long time ago."

"We have to be going," Nora Jane said. "We have people waiting on us."

"May I borrow the photographs to show them?" Freddy took them from Clyda's hand and led Nora Jane toward the back door.

"This is who saved Zandia's life," Clyda was saying. "This is Nora Jane."

"I don't know what to say," Claudine put in. "I brought you a present. Sandy, go get my suitcase, will you?" She was very tall, very thin, nervous and excited. She had picked up Zandia but she was not paying much attention to him. She was trying to figure out what was wrong. "Mother," she added, "get that god-damn cat off the counter, will you? I told you Zandia's allergic to them. Has that cat been inside the whole time?"

"We really have to leave. We'll see you later." Freddy put the photographs into his pocket and he and Nora Jane disappeared through the door.

"I'll call you later," Nora Jane called over her shoulder. "We'll get together later."

They made it through the gate and started up the hill to their house. "Get the girls," she said. "Let's get out of here."

They walked back across the yard, holding hands, tight against each other's bodies. Freddy's shoulders barely came an inch higher than Nora Jane's. "Yet I feel the breadth of them," she said, and he did not ask the meaning. They had grown to talk this way when they were alone together. In sentence fragments, long hints, musings. Perhaps she had learned it from him, or perhaps she had only learned to do it aloud, since she had always whispered parts of secrets to herself and to her cats. Lonely little only child that she had been, always up in trees with a cat, spinning worlds she could inhabit without fear. Now, into this world she had created with this man, a real world of goodness and light, peace and hope, came this moment and they must bear it and survive it.

"He cannot mean to harm us," Freddy answered. "Still,

she is his and he will know it. What do we do now? First we think."

"He thinks they both are his. We should never have kept this secret. Nothing should be a secret. Secrets are dynamite, weapons-grade uranium."

"Who would we have told? Tammili and Lydia? We can't do that."

"Call your mother and tell her we're coming over there. We'll move if we have to. He knows where we live."

"Leave the house?"

"There are millions of houses. Think of the stuff we could throw away."

"All right. Go get the girls. Let's go. A house on the beach. That's what you've always wanted, isn't it?"

"This is what money is for, Freddy. This is the difference in being rich and being poor." They had arrived at the cobbled path that led to the back door. It was sheltered by azalea bushes and they stopped beneath one and moved into each other's arms. Frozen still, on guard, but moving. This was the thing Nieman envied them, this marriage, this shield they had created, the ability to plan and move as one.

Nora Jane disappeared into the house and began to throw clothes for the girls into a suitcase. Freddy got the station wagon out of the garage and drove it to the side door. He went into the living room and turned on the CD player. Then he called his mother. The strains of the Sixth Symphony were in the background while he talked to her. "It's dire, Mother. Someone who is a threat to us is staying next door. We're coming there, for perhaps a week."

"What will you tell the girls?"

"What do you suggest?"

"Say I need them. Say I was frightened."

"You've never been frightened in your life. They'd never believe that."

"Then tell them they can't know."

"I'll say the air-conditioner's broken. Hell, I'll say the power's going off."

"Come on then. I'm waiting."

"We're going to buy another house. Will you go with Nora Jane this afternoon and help her look?"

"Whatever you need."

Ann Harwood hung up the phone and sat staring out the leaded glass doors into the morning light. Then she picked up the phone and called her lover and told him she couldn't drive to the desert as they had planned. "The children need me," she said. "This is why there's no point in getting married."

"Can I help?"

"I don't think so. I'll call you later." She hung up the phone and walked down the hall and began to open doors to unused rooms.

Sandy George Wade stood by himself in Clyda's pink and white guest bedroom feeling the way he had felt most of his life: Frightened, deserted, in the way, waiting for the next blow to fall. I guess I'd like to see those kids she had, he decided. See how they turned out, but what the hell, nobody offered to show them to me, did they?

Zandia came into the room and brandished his plastic sword. Sandy struck a pose and pretended to fence with him. They moved around the room thrusting and pointing at one another. Zandia began to laugh, he ran in little circles, faster and faster, then he jumped up on the bed and held the sword in both hands and began to jump on the mattress. Sandy picked him up and carried him upside down to his mother. "You've been had, Zorro," he said to him. "You've met your match when you fence with Captain Sandy Hook, the master swordsman of the deep." Zandia whacked him on the leg with the sword, then dissolved in upside-down giggles.

Sandy set him upright and took his hand. "Back to Montessori for you, old buddy," he said. "Tomorrow morning bright and early. And this time don't bring home any colds while I'm filming."

*   *   *

Freddy and Lydia had promised to go to movies with Nieman, so only Tammili went with Nora Jane and Ann Harwood to hunt for houses. "I came to California to live by the ocean," Nora Jane said. "I want to live where breakers beat upon the shore. I want to look out the window and see my girls playing in the sand."

"What's she been smoking?" Tammili dissolved in laughter. They were in Ann's Bentley, going to meet a real estate broker. "It's because Zandia fell in the pool, I bet," she added. "She probably wouldn't let us in the ocean if we lived by it."

At five-fifteen that afternoon they found it. A three-story frame house on a promontory where the Pacific Ocean beat against the shore. Nora Jane stood on a slope and watched the waves break against a tall, triangular rock. She walked to the water's edge and watched her footprints come and go. She thought, I did mean to live by the water, where the land meets the sea. "I was on the ocean's edge when I decided you were about to be born," she said to Tammili. "I think you should be excited by the sound of the waves."

"I know. Then you got on the train and went to Willits and that's why we were born there. How many times do I have to hear that story?"

"But do you like the house?" Ann asked. "We'll restore it and paint it and change the landscaping. But the basic plan, the house, how do you feel about it, Tammili?"

"Who wouldn't want that mansion? But I don't want to move. How are we going to get to school? How will Daddy get to work?"

"It isn't that far. We'll keep the other house too. In case we need it. We won't throw it away."

"I don't see how we'll get to school. We'll have to get up at six o'clock in the morning."

"Details," her grandmother said. "Three months and we can have it done. Paint, new bathrooms, new kitchen. I know just the people. I've been wanting to get them some work. This young contractor who's helpful with Planned Parenthood."

"Do you want to see the other two houses?" the real estate agent asked.

"No, we're mad about this house. We'll go back to my house and talk about an offer. Oh, Freddy has to see it. I forgot about that."

"Can we show him tonight?" Nora Jane asked. "Are the lights on?"

"Yes."

"Why are we getting this house?" Tammili asked. "You can tell me the truth. You can trust me."

"Would you wait a few days and let us tell you then?" her grandmother asked. "Could you trust us?"

"Okay. I guess so. But I know why. I know anyway." She walked off from them and stood looking at the house, smirking to herself. They think I'm so dumb. It's because the people next door are anti-Semitic. Dad's afraid they'll be snotty to us or something. He's so protective it's pitiful. Now Grandmother will have to spend a million dollars or something to move us all out here so we won't have any neighbors. It's ridiculous. If they're snotty to me I'll dump the cat litter in their yard. She walked closer to the house. Actually, it was four houses joined together to make one. A colonial house like one in some faraway country in another time. She was drawn to it. She wanted to go back inside and pick out some rooms for herself and Lydia.

"We aren't ever going to tell them or admit it to them," Nora Jane said. "We made up our mind. Can you live with that, Ann? With never letting them know there is any difference in them to you? You have to leave them the same amount of money in your will and things like that. If we keep this from them and they find it out, the older they are when they find out the madder they are going to be. But it's a chance we have to take. I don't want them to meet Sandy. I don't want him trying that charm on them."

"I always knew this, Nora Jane. I didn't know how exactly. I studied science as a girl, you know. I knew Lydia wasn't kin to me, but it's never mattered one way or the other. I adore her. I would rather be her grandmother than any little girl in the world. She's ten times as lovable as Tammili. Tammili reminds me too much of my mother to be able to pull the strings of my heart. Look at her, she's probably going up there to stake out territory. That's what Big Ann would have done. She was a weaver when she got old, did you know that? She had a loom and made twenty or so rugs and we don't know what she did with them. She never gave us one of them. I think she sold them."

"Are you sure you want to buy this house? It costs so much."

"A sound investment. They don't make any more beaches. It would be a good investment if the lot were empty. I might fix it up for myself if you decide you don't want it or Freddy doesn't like it."

"Oh, he'll like it. He'll go crazy. I know his taste. He'll start wanting to fill it with period pieces."

"Let's go find him. We can send Tammili into the movies if they're still at the Octoplex. Were they really going to three movies?"

"Parts of three. That's how Nieman does it, you know. If he comes to one he likes well enough to stay that one gets a review."

II

OF COURSE NIEMAN started seeing the Harwoods' problems as a play. It had everything. Confused passions (the great overbearing winds of the first circle of the Inferno), uncertain parentage, innocence slaughtered, random ill. He was walking around his house listening to Kiri Te Kanawa sing Puccini and thinking of Nora Jane's amazing singing voice, which she almost never let anyone hear. He was musing on the story of her childhood: a father slaughtered in a senseless war, a mother drinking herself into dementia, the portrait of her grandfather in the robes of a supreme court justice, the grandmother in the blue house with the piano and the phonograph records.

"Unfair, unfair, always unfair." Nieman strode around the living room and waved his arms in the air to the music. *Vissi d'arte,* the consolations of art. There was nothing else. Struggle and death, and in the meantime, beauty. Tammili and Lydia and Nora Jane and his best friend, Freddy, who was born to bear the suffering of anyone who came his way. He bore mine, Nieman remembered, when my own father died within a month of his, both taking their cigarette-scarred lungs to the Beth Israel Cemetery. We were fourteen years old but it was Freddy who became the father. It was Freddy who saw to it that our holidays were never sad, Freddy who sent off for the folders and found the wilderness camp where we could learn the things our fathers would have taught us. Freddy who went to Momma and made her let me go. "I won't let him die, Miss Bela," he told her. "I'll see to it personally that Nieman isn't involved in anything that's dangerous. His safety will be more important to me than my own."

Four weeks later they were stuck all night in a canyon in the Sierra Nevada with half the rangers in the area looking for them.

The phone was ringing. It was Freddy, catching Nieman up on the events of the afternoon. "They bought a mansion on the beach. Up by Mendelin Pass. You wouldn't believe what they bought. It looks like Gatsby's house. Mother's in ecstasy, as you can imagine. She's been trying to get me in a house she understands for twenty years. Well, on a higher note, I'm taking two days off for this education jaunt. You want to meet us somewhere or shall we come and pick you up?"

"We all have to be in different buildings at different times. Let's meet at Aranga's at noon and have lunch. I've got to work all night to get caught up. Is that all? They bought a house? You haven't been home?"

"I'm going over later and see if he's left."

"Can I do anything to help?"

"Not yet."

"He has no legal rights. Your name is on the birth certificate, isn't it?"

"We don't want him to know where they are, Nieman. Hide your treasures. You're the one who taught me that. If he sees them he might want them."

"Perhaps you should confront him. Pay him off. Who is he anyway? You need more information. Call Jody and get him to put a tail on him and do a profile. I thought you read murder mysteries."

"That's the best idea you've had. Tammili has decided we are moving to escape anti-Semitism. It's a sore spot with her that she can't experience prejudice."

"The angel. Well, I'll meet you at noon tomorrow. Call Jody Wattes. Get more information. Don't let your imagination run this. Athena's the goddess you need. Balance, knowledge, cool head."

"See you tomorrow then."

Sandy walked around the perimeter of Nora Jane and Freddy's house. It was eight o'clock at night and there were lights on in the living room and central hall but the garage was locked and no one seemed to be there. "They've run off because of me," he said out loud. "Well, I deserve that. I never sent her a penny. I guess they have a good life, her and her Jewish husband and my kids. I wonder what they look like. She always said they might not be mine. What if they were his kids and I'd been supporting them all these years? Well, things will change for me after this picture is released. I'll come see them then." He shook his head. I'll just go up and look around. See what kind of stuff they keep around. You can tell a lot about someone by the things they keep around. Life never lets up on me, does it? If I get happy for fifteen minutes, something comes along to throw me to the mat. Well, I better get back or Claudine will get worried. She's the best thing to come down the pike for me in years. I even like the little kid. Yeah, Zandia's a kick. He's got a criminal mind. And Clyda's okay for an old lady even if she is a nervous wreck. Yeah, Claudine's good for me.

Sandy walked up on the front porch and listened for guard dogs, then tried the door. It opened. In their hurry, Nora Jane and Freddy had left it unlocked. He walked into the foyer and called out, "Anybody here? I brought a message from Clyda next door." He walked into the living room and came face to face with a huge portrait of Tammili when she was nine years old. Her short black hair, her intense, worried black eyes stared out at him. They were in sharp contrast to the frilly white lace dress Nora Jane had made her wear. It was a powerful, no-nonsense face. A forbidding IQ, an analytical mind, a wide, flared nose, the painter had captured them all. It was a portrait of a Medici.

Not very pretty, Sandy decided. She sure doesn't look like me. The face followed him when he tried to turn away. That is not my kid, he decided. It hardly even looks like a kid.

The painting, the empty house, the strangeness of a life he could not imagine, began to work on Sandy's mind. If they were mine they might not like me, he decided. They wouldn't know anything about me. Maybe when the movie comes out I'll send N.J. a print and she can show it to them if she wants to. If they're mine. That kid's not mine. I'm out of here.

He went back out the way that he had come, wiping his prints off the door handle, locking, then unlocking the door. He walked across the yard and climbed over the fence and let himself down into Clyda's backyard. "Where have you been?" Claudine asked. "Zandia's been looking for you. I want to take him down and rent him a video. You want to go with us?"

"I used to know that woman who lives next door," Sandy said. "I knew her in New Orleans. So what are they, rich Jews or something?"

"They run a bookstore," Clyda answered. "I'll go with you to the video store. I need to get out of the house myself."

Claudine sighed. "Well, Momma, I just wanted to get Zandia off to myself for a while. I don't like to have everyone in one car."

The next morning Claudine and Zandia and Sandy got into Claudine's BMW and started driving back to L.A. "I know she got her feelings hurt," Claudine was saying. "But I couldn't take any more. I don't know how I grew up with her working on me morning, noon, and night. It's a wonder I survived. My analyst says it proves what a powerful personality I have that I got away from her. What was all that shit she was telling you about Scientology?"

"She's just lonely, baby. She's an old lady and she's lonely. It was nice of her to keep the kid so long. Don't go bad-mouthing your mother. You should have seen the one I had. When I had one, which wasn't long. I like your old lady. I think she looks good for her age and she leaves you alone."

"Well, it's over. We did it. Let's go home and get back to our own life. That's what I told her. I said, Mother, I have a life of my own, believe it or not, and I need to get back to it." Claudine bent over the wheel, pulled out onto the eight-lane that runs along the coast. "At least it isn't raining."

III

At five minutes to ten on Monday morning Nora Jane was settling into a seat in the back of the history class. A tall man in a gray shirt came into the room and put his books on the professor's desk. He was overweight and soft in the face but he had intelligent eyes and huge black-rimmed glasses and he rolled up his sleeves as he waited for the class to assemble. There were thirty or forty students when all the seats were filled. Nora Jane got out a notebook and a pencil. She began to write. "Walls and foyer, decorator white. Porch ceilings, French blue. Tammili and Lydia's rooms, sunshine yellow, ask them. Go by Goyer's Paints this afternoon."

"Where to begin to talk about the history of the world? How to begin to sort out the threads that led to the Golden Age of Greece and the first historian, Thucydides? Agriculture, the do-mestication of animals, the wheel, pots to store food, ways to carry water, the idea that man has a soul. Where does history begin? Is history a concept of the brain? Does time move in one direction? What is a Zeitgeist? What is an inventor? Is he only a sort of point man, the natural next step created by the force or need of many brains, or is he a lone individual stumbling onto a good idea? What is an idea? Who drilled the first well? Was it a pipe in the ground or a boy or girl sucking moisture from the earth with a straw or reed? Tell me the difference in a hat, a roof, and an umbrella.

"Water, food, shelter, keeping the young alive. Are these the things man needs? When there is an earthquake in San Fran-cisco, what are the first things the survivors do? You do not run into the living room to save the video recorder or the Nikonos.

You run to save the babies. . . ." The professor's voice was deep and soothing. Nora Jane got chills listening to him talk. She was thrilled to be here in this class with her books beside her on the floor. If only Sandy doesn't go over to their school today and kidnap them. They wouldn't go with him. The school wouldn't let them go. I have the mobile phone. I could go out in the hall and call the school. I will in a minute. I have to. I can't stand it.

"Our hold on the earth is tenuous at best," the voice was saying. "It doesn't seem so if you are an English-speaking citizen of the United States of America and don't live in a ghetto. We wake up with our automobiles and jet helicopters and computers and video cameras and houses full of every imaginable sort of thing and we know we have gotten rid of the lions and tigers and bears and wolves and bacteria. Unfortunately we have replaced them with the AIDS virus and antibiotic-resistant tuberculoses, by threats to the very air we breathe and polluted lakes and rivers. Also, the same comets that perhaps destroyed the dinosaurs are aiming at us in the sky. . . ."

"Excuse me," Nora Jane muttered to the girl on her right, and leaving her books, went out into the hall and called the twins' school and talked to the receptionist. "Their grandmother is picking them up at three-thirty," she told the girl. "Mrs. Ann Harwood. She has a pale gray Bentley or else a black Porsche. Don't let them leave with anyone else for any reason. Unless you call me first. Here's the mobile phone number. . . . Okay, I know. Well, thank you."

She went back into the classroom and took her seat and listened to the rest of the lecture. Then she put the books into her backpack and put it on her shoulder and struck out across the campus to find Nieman and Freddy.

Nieman and Freddy were at their designated table at Aranga's waiting for her. "I may sell Clara too," Freddy was saying. "Now that he knows where we are. Of course, Nora Jane always told him they might not be his. The whole time she was pregnant she told him that. Isn't that just like her, the darling. Of course the thing is he's AB positive and so am I and so are both of them. It's such a bizarre coincidence."

"Is he bright enough to remember all that and call it into play? I thought he drank."

"Well, obviously he doesn't anymore for what it's worth. He's bright, Nieman. Lydia tests at 13o. Just because she's not as smart as Tammili. Of course, psychopathic personalities are never dumb. That's been proven." Freddy played with his coffee cup. "I hope she's all right. Where is she? She got out at eleven."

"It's ten after eleven. Maybe you should prepare to buy him off. I hate to keep bringing this up, but you could just offer him money."

"Solicit blackmail? So we can spend the rest of our days wondering when he'll show up wanting more? It's frightening, Nieman. We can't know what he's thinking. What he's up to."

IV

"I don't know why that woman who saved him never came back to get the present," Claudine was saying. They had stopped at San Jose to get lunch and were still on the road. Claudine was driving and Sandy was watching Zandia and manning the CD player. "Two ounces of Joy I bought her. I wish I'd just taken it home with me. I thought she was rude, didn't you? I keep thinking they think I'll sue for letting him fall in. I keep reading fear of lawsuits, don't you? Did you see the way they beat it out of there?"

"I told you, I used to know her. Maybe there's something she doesn't want her husband to know that she thinks I'll tell him."

"She had a bad reputation, huh?"

"I didn't really know her. She just went to our church. Well, that's over, baby. You're right about one thing. If your mother wants to see the kid she can come and visit us."

"If she ever saw our condo maybe she'd buy me a bigger one. She's got tons of money but her shrink tells her not to give it to me. I hate his guts, the son-of-a-bitch."

"Think about something good. You're making wrinkles, baby, worrying about things like that. We've got plenty going on. I hope that deal down in Mexico works out. We could have a lot of fun living down there for a while. I love it down there. The more I think about it, the more I think it's a breakthrough script for you."

"Sandy, Sandy, Sandy," Zandia yelled from the car seat. "Sandy, Sandy, Sandy."

"He's crazy about you," Claudine said. "I think he likes you better than he does me."

Later that afternoon, while Claudine was at the store, Sandy found a piece of stationery and wrote a letter to Nora Jane.

> Dear N.J.,
>
> It was really good to see you looking so happy. Your husband looks like a nice guy. You shouldn't have run off like that. I saw you leave. I thought, there she goes. She always did think she was invisible when she had her head in the sand.
>
> Don't worry about me, baby. I'm glad you got a life. I got one too. We're doing a film in Mexico as soon as we finish this one.
>
> Thanks for saving Zandia. I really like this kid even if I do wish sometimes the little helicopter blade on his hat would fly him off to cloud land for a couple of weeks. Around here we call him IN YOUR FACE.
>
> Take care of yourself. Love always,
>
> Sandy

He carried the letter around for a couple of days, then he tore it up.

Freddy Harwood called his old friend Jody Wattes, who had given up a profitable law practice to be a private investigator, and asked him to put a tail on Sandy. Then he and Nora Jane and Tammili and Lydia moved back into their house while they waited for the new one to be renovated.

"I still don't know why we went over to Grandmother's to begin with," Tammili was saying. "Or why all of a sudden we have to have a house on the beach. It's because the neighborhood is anti-Semitic, isn't it? You just don't want us to know. I don't think people should move because of things like that. So is that what's going on?"

"No, it is not." Nora Jane was doing all the lying on this

matter. Not that she was good at it, but she was better than Freddy was. "I have always wanted a house on the beach. I never really liked this house. This house is pure nineteen seventy. I want to look out a window and see you playing on a beach. If we are going to live near an ocean, we might as well live on it."

"We want room to grow and change," Freddy added. "We might want some foreign exchange students. More dogs. Anything can happen. Besides, think how happy it is making Grandmother Ann."

"I'll have to get up at six in the morning to get to school."

"Maybe you'll want to change schools in the next few years. We'll go and look at some. You might want to go to a different school that's closer."

"You aren't telling me." Tammili stood with her hands on her hips.

"We're evolving," Freddy said. "Rilke said, You must change your life. Are you afraid to live in a different house, Tammili?"

"No. I just want to know what's going on. You all are up to something and I want to know what it is. Grandmother's getting married to that guy, isn't she? Is that it?"

"I doubt it," Freddy answered. "It wouldn't be like her to get married."

Nora Jane went to her daughter and put her arm around her shoulders. "Your college student mother is going to write a report on the new cave they found in France. Come help me pull up the data on the computer. Will you do that?"

"They told us about it." Tammili got excited. "They showed us a picture of the paintings. There was a herd of animals so good no one could paint it any better. I almost fainted. They showed it to us today in art class. You had that too? They talked about it in college?"

"Uncle Nieman knows about it." Lydia had come into the room from the shadow of the door where she had been listening. "Uncle Nieman's been inside the one at Lascaux. He's one of the few people in America who ever got to see it."

"It was a religion." Tammili took her mother's hand, began to lead her in the direction of the room with the computer. "They weren't very big or they couldn't have fit through the crawl spaces. I bet they weren't any bigger than Lydia and me. I can't believe you guys are going to college. It's amazing. Come on. I know exactly where to find it. It was all in the newspapers a while ago. Uncle Nieman made me copies of the stories. I've got them in my room somewhere."

Lydia and Tammili and Nora Jane disappeared in the direction of the computer and Freddy walked out onto the patio and looked up at the stars and started making deals. Just keep them safe, he offered. That's all. Name your price. I'm ready. Don't I always keep my word? Have I ever let you down?

Going to live on the beach, his father answered. Well, that's all right until the big storms come.

What's it like up there? Freddy asked.

I don't know, his father answered. I'm too busy watching you to care.

On the Problem of Turbulence

"Where were we ten years ago, that's what I have to remember," Nora Jane Harwood said to herself many times during those terrible days of April.

"'Natural flowing shapes,'" Nieman Gluuk consoled himself by musing. "'Great rivers meander in wide curves to the sea. In the sea itself the Gulf Stream meanders, making loops, swinging east and west. Great rivers of warm and cold water fight in the sea.' As Schwenk says, 'the flow wants to realize itself regardless of the surrounding material.' You cannot fight these powers. But it does not mean we're doomed. We could learn to ride on the waves as surfers. . . ."

"Chaos," Freddy Harwood said to them both, wiping his glasses on his sweater, then pushing them back onto his face. "Toni Morrison's house burns down weeks after she wins the Nobel, children are bombed and starved, Mother goes out with that fool, sects surround us, so dark and so many, we cannot even discern the enemy. The enemy is everywhere and is still what it was three thousand years ago. Ignorance reigns, is fed and breeds. . . . 'The best lack all conviction while the worst are full of passionate intensity.' Yeats."

"Don't wear yellow when I wear yellow," Tammili said to her twin sister, Lydia. "You always copy me."

"I didn't see you wearing yellow," Lydia lied. *"I was in the other room. It's a coincidence."*

"Stop talking like Nieman. You just try to use the words he gives us."

"Well, so what? That's what they're for. Dad said so. He said any word you use belongs to you. I'm not afraid to say coincidence out loud."

Nine-fifteen in the morning. April one, nineteen hundred and ninety-five.

Freddy Harwood sat at his desk in his office at Clara Books and thought about the past. The great days of Berkeley were over and there were those who said they would never come again. Freddy harbored a secret hope that they would come again. They might ride in on a revival of artistic freedom, a cure for AIDS might do the trick, one great stage play, new musical forms, a poet who could break the heart and make the soul sing.

There had been the Stephen Mitchell translations of Rilke, that had seemed a breakthrough, the Danish novels of Peter Hoeg, Kilain Alter's biography of Francis Alter. Other sightings. All was not lost.

Freddy got up from his desk and wandered down into the pre-opening activity of the bookstore. He had dropped his daughters off at school, then gone to the store to begin sorting invoices for the spring books. It was a task he never minded doing. It was what he was doing the night Nora Jane walked into his life. My Nora, he thought, my life, my hope, my meaning. Freddy Harwood adored his wife and children. He loved them in a manner that seems old-fashioned in a cynical world. He lived to serve and protect them. Each act of his day was measured against his concern for their happiness and well-being. In his soul Freddy believed other men felt the same way about their families. He could no longer tolerate the knowledge of cruelty. Stories of wife and child abuse affected him so deeply he had stopped reading newspapers. His secretary, Frances, read them for him and told him what they said.

"I read books," he defended himself by saying. "Sooner or later anything worth reading will make it into a book."

The books that were on his desk at the moment included two translations of the *Paradiso*, one by Mark Musa and one by Charles Singleton, *Fima*, by Amos Oz, *United States*, by Gore Vidal, a book of essays by Robert Penn Warren, and the *Selected Letters of Philip Larkin*.

Freddy Harwood had always been a sweet man. Now, in his forties, he had become a saint. Wise men and women sought him out. On any Saturday night his living room was filled with the best minds who lived in or passed through the Berkeley area. Last week it had been Abraham Pais and his son. Tonight it would be the great editor Sebranek Conrad and his companion, the novelist Adrien Searle. Nora Jane was a big fan of Ms. Searle's writings and had been up all night the night before rereading her books.

Freddy's secretary, Frances, cornered him by a stack of cookbooks. "It's ridiculous to have a reading at noon," she said. "We've tried this before and no one came. I had an appointment at the doctor but I canceled it."

"They'll turn out. Her fans are loyal. Sebranek called last night and said they'd be here about eleven to sign stock. Do you have the reading space set up?"

"Yes. Well, he's the grand old man of publishing now. I want to thank him for not selling out. He's never put his imprint on a book he was ashamed of publishing."

"Now I'm worried no one will come. Go in the office, Frances, and call the list of poets and some of Mother's friends. Do it now."

"There're seventy pre-orders. It'll be fine. We always think no one is coming."

"Someday no one will. This is an idea that has outlived its time. It's turned into souvenir collecting. Well, let's make it as painless for Ms. Searle as possible." He began to straighten the books on a sale table. He set aside some hardback copies of *Brazzaville Beach*. "Put these by the cash register with the new books. People should read this book."

"There's no more room."
"Make room."

In their crazy outgrown glass and timber house overlooking the bay, Nora Jane was walking around the living room listening to an Italian grammar tape and picking up things the twins had left behind. There was a lunch box with a peanut butter sandwich untouched in its plastic bag. There was a fuchsia scarf Lydia was currently tying around her ponytail. There was a Barbie doll dressed for scuba diving, a plate of nachos, a copy of *Little House on the Prairie* with UGH written on the cover by Tammili. The UGH had been marked out with a red Magic Marker. Under it Lydia had written EXCELLENT.

Nora Jane gathered all the things into a wicker basket and carried it to the kitchen and then went into her room to dress for the day. She was missing two classes at Berkeley today and she was keeping a crazy, scary secret.

After ten years of never getting pregnant again and wanting to, she was three days late. Drugstore test kits had confirmed it. I can't tell him until I know for sure, she decided. I can't even mention this unless it's certain. He would go crazy. I don't even want to bring it up. He won't notice. He's involved with Sebranek's coming and Ms. Searle.

She looked at herself in the mirror. Put her hand to her mouth. Began to chew on her fingers. Then she left the mirror and began to run water into the tub. Then she began to sing.

A passerby might have thought a great diva was in the tub as the opening notes of "Quando m'en vo'soletta" began to fill the room. When Nora Jane sang to herself she was always alone with her grandmother Lydia, in the long hot days of summer, in New Orleans, Louisiana, in the part of her childhood that she treasured and could bear to remember. Mirlitons were growing on the fence behind her grandmother's house. A morning glory vine twined around the pillars of the porch. It was fragrant and divine and her grandmother Lydia there beside her to save her from her mother and all the other evils of the world.

*   *   *

Nora Jane stepped into the tub of hot water and sank down below the waves. Don't think about New Orleans, she told herself. The past is a swamp. Adrien Searle is coming to the store and we get to take her out to lunch. Not to mention telling Freddy about this baby.

Nora Jane sank back into the waves. She was in her first semester at college so the timing would be the way things usually end up happening. The minute you forget about wanting something it shows up.

I have to be careful telling Freddy. If he acts too happy it might make the girls jealous. I don't want them jealous of some little baby before it's even born. What if it was a little boy as crazy as Freddy? Or as handsome as my father. She shook her head and got out of the tub and started drying herself.

Well, I have to tell him today. I have to stop being so secretive about things. I'm as bad as I was when I was young.

She went into the bedroom and pulled on a pair of slacks and a blue and white striped polo shirt. She ran a comb through her hair, found her car keys, and ran. She pulled out of the garage in her little red Miata and headed toward the expressway. I should eat something, she decided. You can't go around skipping breakfast when you're pregnant. She pulled off the highway at McDonald's and ordered a sausage biscuit and a cup of orange juice and ate them as she drove. It was ten-thirty. If she hurried she would have time to tell him before the reading.

He's so crazy, she decided. It's absurd to like your husband as much as I like him. But I wish he wouldn't worry about things. He'll find a way to worry about this pregnancy. He'll read about a hundred books. He'll probably sign us up for some of those dopey parenting courses. Well, I'm not going.

She found a parking place behind the store and went in the back and found Freddy by the cash register, rearranging books.

"Thanks for coming down early. How are you?" He smiled his dazzling smile.

"I have to talk to you right away. Come in the office."

"Oh, God, is it something about the girls?"

"No. It's something good. At least I think it's good. Come on. Hurry up." She took his arm and led him up the stairs to his office. She shut the door and stood holding it. "I'm pregnant," she said. "I'm pretty sure. I did two drugstore tests. I think it's true. I'm pretty sure."

"Oh, God, my darling one." He went to her and took her in his arms. Then he began to cry. Laughing and crying.

"Don't you dare cry. Oh, God, I knew this was going to happen. That's why I didn't tell you last night."

"You knew this last night and you didn't tell me?"

"I wanted to wait one more day. And do a second test."

"I knew this. I dreamed it last night. I had this little boy and I was holding his hand. We were in a valley. At the foot of some mountains."

"You did not. You did not dream this. And we don't know if it's a girl or a boy." Now she was laughing too. They were leaning on Freddy's desk, laughing as if they knew the funniest thing in the world.

Sebranek Conrad had become a great man, almost by accident. He had not sought out greatness. He had just been a scrawny hardworking kid from upstate New York who had dreamed of going into publishing. His neighbor in the village of Rhinebeck, New York, was a publisher, a man whose family owned a publishing house in Boston. When Sebranek was a teenager he had done odd jobs for this man in the summers. He had chopped wood, cleaned barns, groomed horses, planted trees, mended fences, always side by side with the talkative Irishman. Often, as he grew older, the man would have him to the house to meet visiting authors. Sometimes the authors would work by their side. Hemingway had come to the farm and John Fowles had been a visitor one summer. Sebranek had grown up knowing writers and was fascinated by the world they inhabited.

He had worked his way through Yale and done well there, graduating magna cum laude and with other honors. Afterward he had gone to work for a publishing house in New York owned by one of the men he had met on his mentor's farm. By the time he was forty he was a senior editor. By the time he was fifty he was editor in chief.

"I was lucky to be there in those years," he was fond of saying.

"At the end of publishing as we knew it. I was there and I'm still there and will be to the end. Adrien and I are holding on very well, thank you."

He looked across the room at the sleeping body of his lady love, the feared feminist writer Adrien Searle. She was sleeping on her side, curled up like a child. She could sleep anywhere. She never woke at dawn to worry about the day. She lay down beside him and did not stir for eight or nine or ten hours. This fascinated Sebranek and he envied it. When they were younger he would sometimes wake her in the middle of the night and ask her what time it was. She would answer to within a minute of the time and go immediately back to sleep.

"We should be married," he said to himself. "She should give in on that. At least she could have my insurance and my social security." He rubbed his eye with his hand, straightened out a kink in his neck, felt his glasses bearing down on the bridge of his nose. Sixty-four was all right but not as good for traveling as it once had been. Well, she had wanted him along and he had come. *Mission,* her new book was called, and she swore it was her last.

He walked across the room and sat down on the edge of the bed. "We need to get up now," he said. He lay down beside her. He began to caress her arms and breasts. Kissed her soft hair. She woke and started giggling. "You're too old for this," she said. "I know I'm too old for it. Take your clothes off, please. Just this once more and then I'm giving this up forever. Hurry up, it's your absolute last chance to make love to me."

Later, while they were dressing, she brought up the thing they didn't want to talk about. "Do you think Johnnie will come?"

"No."

"Do you think he will even call?"

"It's been in the papers and I had my secretary call and tell him we were here. He knows where we are. He would have called the hotel if he wanted to see us."

"Why didn't you call him yourself?"

"I tried to. He doesn't have a phone. You have to leave messages at some service. He doesn't talk to me on the phone. You know that. If he contacts me at all it's an undated note with no address. He's in full retreat, Adrien. There's nothing I can do."

"Well, this is his territory now. In a way we're invading his territory."

"Ungrateful sons who don't speak to me don't have territory as far as I'm concerned."

"At least he stopped taking drugs."

"We assume he stopped. Don't worry about Johnnie, Adrien. Worry about your poor old starving editor. I need to eat breakfast before I face this crowd."

"Do you think there will be a crowd?"

"Of course there will be. Your fans love you. Well, come along. You look fine. I'm starving. Let's leave this room."

They had a quick breakfast in the hotel cafe, then a car came to pick them up and delivered them at two minutes past eleven to Clara Books. Sebranek took Adrien's arm and they walked into a sea of admiring fans. Adrien was wearing a yellow sweater and gold earrings. Her hair was a riot of dark gold curls. Her smile was honest, her courtesy unfailing. "Thank you for coming here," she was saying. "I'm so pleased to be here. So pleased to get to know you."

Sebranek left her to her fans and joined Freddy by the front cash register. They were old compadres of several battles. When Sebranek first published Salman Rushdie, Freddy had been the only bookstore in Berkeley to display the books in his front window. Clara had been bombed in retaliation for that. Freddy had rebuilt the front windows and put the books back in them. The store had been bombed on Wednesday. By Saturday afternoon the windows were repaired and the Rushdie books were in both of them.

"How's the book tour?" Freddy asked. "Are you sorry you started this?"

"It's only three cities. I'm enjoying myself. It's a revelation, to tell the truth. More publishers should go to bookstores. Maybe I'll start accompanying all my authors."

A line had formed of people trying to get into the room

where Adrien was going to read. Freddy and Sebranek watched the people for a while, stopping every now and then to talk to someone who came their way. There was only one front entrance. Neither of them saw Johnnie come in. He was a familiar figure to Freddy. Just because he was in full retreat from his family didn't mean he had stopped reading books.

Adrien read the first twenty pages of her book. Then the audience asked her questions. They were hesitant, silly questions at first, but, as she seemed to give of herself with good humor, the questions became more serious.

Johnnie walked around the edge of the crowd. He was wearing a coarse beige jacket and a pair of shorts. His hair was cut as short as a Marine recruit's. He had a backpack full of books over one arm. He was taller than Sebranek and handsomer. He looked like Northern California. He looked like Northern California had been invented for him.

"Are you reading any contemporary poets?" he asked Adrien when she recognized him and pointed his way. "Is there anyone new you can tell us about?"

"I should ask you to tell me," she answered. "I don't haunt bookstores as I used to. I used to ferret out writers, find poems. I was looking for them, I was on the prowl for writing and now I am like a domesticated wolf. I eat and sleep and write and watch movies and stay home and wait for things to come to me. Perhaps I'll spend the afternoon searching this bookstore and the next time someone asks me that I'll have a better answer."

"Have you read Michael Atkinson?" a young girl asked. Then the audience joined in and began to tell each other about poets. Sebranek saw his chance and went to his son and embraced him. "Thanks for coming," he said. "I don't know if you got any of the messages."

"I can't stay long. I just came by to say hello. I have a meeting in an hour that I can't miss. I'm involved in something I want to talk to you about soon, Dad. I can't talk about it yet. But I may need your help with it soon." Johnnie moved back into the children's section. His father followed, reaching for his billfold, taking out money.

"Stay and have lunch with us. It's just Freddy and Adrien and myself. Or perhaps we can see you later."

"Don't give me that. I don't want money." Sebranek was pushing a hundred-dollar bill into Johnnie's pocket. "Don't do that, Dad. I'm a grown man."

"I want to give you something. I want to do something. I don't want this rift between us. Your mother and I are on good terms. Why can't you and I be? We need to spend some time together. I'm coming back out here in July. We could go to the Oregon coast or climb a mountain. Will you think about it?"

"Sure. I have to leave now, Dad. I really have to be somewhere in half an hour. I want to talk to you. I'll call you next week when you get back." Johnnie was moving toward the door, still facing his father. Behind them the crowd had surrounded Adrien and she was signing books.

"What are you doing? Are you working? What's going on?"

"No time now, I'll tell you later. When I get it squared away. It's still in limbo. Well, you look great, Dad. So does Adrien. I'll buy the book when I have time and read it." He stopped and allowed Sebranek to embrace him, then he was gone, out the turnstile and onto Telegraph Avenue, and his father followed him and watched him down the street. His youngest son, tall, proud, arrogant, who had once been a sickly, asthmatic child coughing his way around the streets of Brooklyn. It was easy to see how the transformation had occurred. The same hard will had driven the child that seemed to drive the man. We don't know them when they are grown, Sebranek told himself. They go off and become a mystery to us. If they would let us in we would not understand what we were seeing. "For their souls dwell in the house of tomorrow, which you cannot visit, not even in your dreams." *The Prophet.* We cannot walk in their shoes nor save them from sorrow. Parallel worlds, enigmas. So be it.

Johnnie caught a streetcar and took it to the last stop. He got off and walked the next two miles to an abandoned warehouse where he and four other young people had made an after-school hangout for deserted and homeless kids. He threw his book bag into a corner and dragged the ladder out onto the floor and began to put a new net on the basketball goal. He had stopped on his way to the streetcar and bought it with the hundred-dollar bill Sebranek had stuffed in his pocket. The rest he had spent on parts for the stove. "I'll fix that stove as soon as I finish here," he told the redheaded girl who stood with her hands on her hips watching him. "You'll be baking cookies by the time school is out."

"So did you see your dad?"

"Yep. He bought this net. What did you find out about the lease?"

"He'll extend it if we repair the bathroom. It's going to cost six or seven hundred dollars to do that. Connie said she'll put in five hundred from her dividend check but that won't pay for all of it. I'll get a job if I have to."

"You have a job." Johnnie took off his jacket. He reached in the pockets reflexively. There were three more hundred-dollar bills folded together. "That son-of-a-bitch," he said. "That god-damn controlling bastard."

When the last book was signed and the last fan listened to, Nora Jane drove Sebranek and Adrien to Chez Panisse. Freddy was following in his car. "He doesn't like to wait at Chez Panisse," Nora Jane explained. "He has this thing with them that's been going on for years. He can't believe they won't give him a table when they say they're going to. But he loves the food so much he has to eat there. It's better if he comes after we get a table. It's so volatile between him and the maître d'. Well, they have these goat cheese pastries that are worth any wait."

"I've been there," Adrien said. "I used to stay in Berkeley in the fall. I had some friends who lived here."

They were in Nora Jane's convertible. Sebranek was in the front seat. Adrien was squeezed into the back. She picked up a book from the floor. It was *Little House in the Big Woods*. "Is this good? I've never read these books."

"Lydia loves them and Tammili hates them. They're fraternal twins, you know. Do you know about them? Our daughters?"

"I heard that Freddy delivered them in a house in the woods under terrible circumstances and a helicopter came and there was a big rescue and everyone lived. That's Sebranek's version."

"That's it. Then we got married and here we are. Well, Freddy hates the story now. He thinks the girls will hear it when they grow up and think they were in danger because we were counterculture people or something. One minute he's so liberal and the next he's as conservative as the pope."

"Sebranek does that." Adrien laughed.

"Every six months I beg her to marry me in a church."

"Why don't you do it?"

"I don't know why we don't. Maybe I think it would end up in *People* magazine. My love turned into a *People* anecdote."

Nora Jane swerved to avoid a truck, then swerved back to the center. "Don't worry about a thing," she said. "I've never had a wreck in my life." She turned into the street of the restaurant, drove smartly down three blocks, expertly backed into a parking place, and turned off the motor.

They went into the restaurant and settled down to wait in a rattan-furnished lounge. Its windows looked out upon a garden and a street. The smells from the kitchen were subtle, rich, pungent, clean. Light fell down through the shuttered windows and the skylights. Palm fronds moved in the breeze from the air-conditioning vents. "Freddy said you bought Salman Rushdie's apartment in New York," Nora Jane said. "That's so brave of you. I'd like to know about it if it's something you can talk about."

"We benefited from that, not him." Sebranek put his arm around the back of the wicker love seat, uncrossed his legs. "It's a dream apartment, overlooking Central Park. Something I'd never have been able to afford. I had trouble adjusting to that part of town at first, but Adrien loves it. She likes grandeur."

"It's a mixed blessing." Adrien smiled at her. "I feel like we're at ground zero in that place. It's beautiful and comfortable but sometimes it seems we really aren't in New York City. It's the Middle East, in the heart of feuds so ancient and bloody that anything which touches them is spoiled. Too many dead on both sides. Husbands, fathers, brothers, sisters, mothers. I had it redecorated, the old wallpaper removed, floors redone. Still, it's the place where Salman lived. Nothing changes that."

"I couldn't read his books." Nora Jane sighed, her old Southern politeness making her cautious. "I think they're boring and overwritten, or just plain silly. It's terrible that they want to kill him, but if they'd left him alone no one would have read the books. Well, that's just my opinion."

"I wonder what he thinks of his own writings. I don't suppose he has much objectivity. Not that any writer has much."

"Salman is a line drawn in the sand." Sebranek spread his hands on his knees. "I'm going to talk about him at a conference of newspaper editors next week. He's having a hell of a life. They made their point with him, that's for sure. They have killed two of his translators."

"This has made a battlefield of literature," Adrien added.

"Free speech is always a battlefield. Always was, always will be. I wish Freddy was here. I want to talk to him about this while I have it on my mind."

"What do you do, Nora Jane?" Adrien asked. "Do you help Freddy with the store?"

"I've gone back to school to get a degree. I was going to study sociology but I think I'll go on and be in the music department instead. My grandmother was a diva. I took lessons when I was young from a man in New Orleans who was really good. I just never have liked to sing in public. So I decided it was all right to go on and study it for myself. Anyway, I just found out I'm pregnant, so that changes things. We didn't plan it. I guess you think we're crazy, having children in this crowded world. Anyway, we're having it."

"No one should be without their art." Adrien reached over and touched Nora Jane's hand. "Being pregnant shouldn't interfere with music in any way. It might make your voice better. I have a friend in San Francisco who is one of the greatest teachers in the world. She taught Kathleen Battle. She lives out here because she makes money coaching people for the movies. Delaney Hawk is her name. Have you heard of her? If you could pay her, she would teach you."

"God, yes. Everyone knows about her."

"Your speaking voice is lovely. I can imagine how well you might sing. I was telling Sebranek a while ago that your voice was wonderful, wasn't I, my darling?"

"She was indeed. She's mad for accents and voices."

"I'd love to meet Mrs. Hawk. Would you take me there?"

"We'll go tomorrow. I need to see her myself. I'll call her this afternoon."

The maître d' came to take them to a table. As they were being seated, Freddy joined them, carrying more books for Adrien to sign and a box wrapped in white satin paper and tied with a velvet ribbon. "We found these books in my office. I forgot to give them to Frances. Would you mind signing five more for us?" He handed the books to Adrien, then pulled out a chair next to Nora Jane and handed her the package.

"You just didn't want to wait for a table." She took the package and laid it beside her napkin. "What is this? Where did you get a present for me so fast?"

"It was for your birthday. Now it's for the baby. Please open it."

She removed the ribbon and the paper. Inside was a velvet case. Inside the case was a diamond bracelet. Twenty small perfect diamonds in gold links. "Oh, my God," she said. "Freddy, take this back. I don't have any use for this. Where would I wear something like this?"

"They were Grandmother's. All I paid for was the setting. If you don't want it, save it for the girls."

"Of course she wants it." Adrien picked up the bracelet and held it out. "Let me put it on your arm. Diamonds and babies, a cause for celebration. Order some wine, Sebranek. It's a finite world. Let's celebrate this day."

Sebranek signaled a waiter. "I wish Johnnie could have stayed to be with us. He looked fine, didn't you think so? His mother is the passive-aggressive resentment queen of the East Coast," he said to Freddy. "It's driven him to extremes."

"Good wombs have borne bad sons, and vice versa." Adrien touched his arm.

"Don't say that in front of me." Nora Jane laughed. "What if I was carrying a bad one."

"Johnnie isn't bad," Sebranek said. "He's just confused and can't decide what to do with his life. I don't know what he's doing for a living. I guess his mother sends him money. He's always been able to manipulate her. Well, what can I do but love him and wait?"

"You can't fix their lives for them. I wrote a piece for *Elle* last year about parenting grown children. I learned something from writing it. I had a great mother. She liked being a mother and she was healthy and protective. A psychiatrist told me a lovely thing. She said a great mother produces an irrational sense of security in a child. I'm irrationally secure. That's why I can do such an insecure thing for a living. Once I wrote three mediocre, almost bad, books in a row and still I kept on believing I was a good writer."

"They weren't bad." Sebranek laughed. "I liked them enough to publish them, before I fell in love with her."

"You were probably always in love with her," Freddy added, and they all laughed at that. "I was in love with her for weeks when I read *Dark Winter*."

Nora Jane was quiet, thinking of her own drunken mother, her lonely nights, her dirty house. Nothing like that will ever happen to my children, she thought grimly. I guess I better quit school. I can't do that with this baby coming. I can read books. I don't have to go to college to be happy.

"Nora Jane is the best mother in the world," Freddy said. "She's stood in there and learned and been firm and sweet at the same time. If I'd had her I'd probably be the president by now. Our girls aren't perfect but they do well in school and they're happy, I think."

"They're ten years old," Nora Jane added. "They are so funny. They like being twins but then they have spells of not wanting anyone to know it. Lydia is the one who likes the twin thing. Tammili, who is like Freddy, is always straining against it. They're wonderful to have. We like them a lot."

The waiter brought wine and food. They ate and drank. The conversation moved on to lighter subjects. When they parted, Adrien and Nora Jane made plans to go the next afternoon to pay a call on Delaney Hawk. "You will profit from knowing her whether she accepts you as a student or not," Adrien said. "She adores money and probably won't be able to turn down a student who is sure to pay. I have a premonition about your meeting her. Something portentous in the wind."

"You aren't coming to dinner tonight?" Freddy asked. "My friend Nieman is dying to meet you."

"I promised her the ballet," Sebranek answered. "I do anything for my authors, didn't you know?"

II

The Muslim fundamentalist sect to which Navin Backer belonged was not closely aligned with the group that blew up the World Trade Center but it was sympathetic to it. The old sheikh who was standing trial in New York City was a sentimental favorite with the young men who came each day to the house on Telegraph Avenue and sat around drinking coffee, watching television and reading Iraqi newspapers brought in on the daily planes from Paris and Madrid. The papers were brought in by a service that also supplied them with money and explosive devices.

Navin was in a dark mood. His number two wife was sulky and after three years had not produced a child and his number one wife had become so fat she no longer interested him. He wanted to go home to Baghdad and get new wives and walk along streets where men and women did not view him with disdain. He had been in a dark mood all spring. Now his mood had turned vicious.

"He needs something to do to take his mind off his wives," his mentor, Amir Haven, told his second in command. "We must send him to blow up an airplane or a boat. Is there nothing for young Navin to make him bloom?"

Both men laughed. "Why not two airplanes, perhaps the whole airport, anything to get his mind off women," the second in command jokingly suggested.

"Here is an interesting thing in the newspaper. This Sebranek

Conrad. Isn't he on the list? I've heard him mentioned. Is he the one who is going to publish the books of the whore?"

"Let me see." Amir took up the paper and read the short piece in the Book Talk section. Then he went to his desk and rummaged through his papers and found the name. "What is the bookstore named?"

"Clara."

"We bombed it ten years ago when the heretic published the book he hasn't been punished for yet. Yes, that might interest Navin. We could send him to demonstrate or throw a brick through the window. Something useful but not too daring. Dangerous but not important enough to call attention to us at this time. Bring him in here. Let me talk to him."

Amir sat back in his chair. He had no interest in taking foolish chances, but still, this might be useful in several ways. He considered the idea. A book publisher was not high profile with the general public but it scared an influential group. It was always difficult to decide who to target. A hit should send out waves, like a pebble dropped into a pond. It should be unexpected, fresh, but with the message clear. This might do to remind people they were there, that men of God would not tolerate the insults the godless heaped upon them. Also, it would keep the young men busy. Their lives were not good in the United States. They were spat upon in the eyes of the women. He had felt it himself. Felt his sexual organs shrink at their piggish soft-faced looks, their contemptuous gazes. The community was not organized. They were spread around the city, some in disguise as teachers and Christians, others working at menial jobs. The women were affected also. At first they were frightened by the supermarkets and automobiles, then you could almost hear it happening, as their curiosity began to overpower their modesty and training. This was all a bad thing, this being in America, even if it did ensure a heavenly reward. But I do not always believe that Allah cares, Amir thought. I am not sure Allah exists in this land. Perhaps he cannot see through the smoke that drifts above their houses. Perhaps he is too offended by their ways to turn his head in this direction. Allah be praised. Forgive a humble servant.

Navin came into the room and made obeisance. Then he stood against the wall. Navin didn't like to sit in chairs. Even in America he liked to pretend he was on the desert. He confronted the universe at every moment. He imagined wind and sand in his face.

"I think we will remind them that we are watching," Amir said, spreading the newspaper out on the desk. Pointing to the article. "All the Jews are not in Israel."

"As Allah knows."

"Would you like to be the messenger?"

"If I am needed. The list of enemies is long."

"For now we will not make it shorter but we will frighten them perhaps. Would you like to leave a message for this man?" Navin moved across the room, looked down at the newspaper. "A small explosion in a bookstore window perhaps," Amir continued. "A hotel room in disarray. What do you see happening?"

"Give me a driver. I will disturb their peace before they leave the city."

"Allah is pleased."

"Allah is Allah. I am unworthy to say his name."

After lunch Freddy went back to the store and Nora Jane returned home and sat on the steps waiting for the twins. She was trying to decide how to tell them about the baby. She stretched her legs out in front of her. The sun beat down and bounced off the stone and warmed and soothed her. They are so different, she was thinking, remembering the girls leaving for school that morning, dressed as though they were continents apart. Lydia in tomboy clothes and tennis shoes, Tammili in a serious jumper and starched white blouse.

A station wagon pulled into the driveway and the girls got out. Lydia dragging a pink backpack behind her. Tammili with her pack sitting squarely on her shoulders.

"I'm going to meet a singing teacher tomorrow," Nora Jane said, when they were near enough to hear.

"Then you'll go on the stage and we'll never see you again."

Lydia abandoned her backpack altogether and went to her mother and cuddled up beside her on the stairs.

"That's good," Tammili said. "That's good, Mother. That would be good for you."

"What did you do in school?"

"We had a Spanish festival with this stupid piñata. I'm about sick of this multicultural stuff. Miss Armand had on this long skirt. All we do is waste time. I'll never get into Harvard going to Country Day. If you don't get me in a better school, I'm going to quit and just stay home."

"She asked Miss Armand if she could go to the library while they had the festival." Lydia looked at her mother and raised her eyes as if to say, Only you and I know what this means.

"And did they let you, Tammili?"

"Part of the time they did. They made me stay for the songs. But at least I didn't have to waste my time on the stupid piñata. I'm going to tell Uncle Nieman about it. He thinks it's hilarious the stuff they do." Tammili carefully removed her backpack and got out three papers with A's on them and handed them over. "I got the highest grade in the class in math."

"You always do," Lydia added. "So what?"

Uncle Nieman was their godfather, and he took his godfathering seriously. He saw them at least twice a week, to check, he said, on their spiritual progress, by which he meant what they were reading and what movies they were seeing. He had given them leather-bound editions of the Harvard Classics for their eighth birthday and also kept them supplied with videos he thought suitable. Not only did he buy them books and films, he lectured them on the things he bought. At the moment they were studying *Green Mansions*, which he read aloud to them when he came to dinner on Friday nights.

When the girls had eaten a snack and gone off on their bikes, Nora Jane went into the music room and opened the piano and began to play. She lifted her head and began to practice scales. Her voice had lost nothing in the years she had ignored it. If anything it was even sweeter and clearer, with a range that was almost unearthly at times. Since she had never strained it or challenged it, it was still a young voice, as natural and beautiful as a bird's song. It was the one thing she had always kept to herself. She had never let anyone persuade her to use her voice for anything except the joy of singing when she felt like singing. My voice is not for sale, she had always said to herself, even in the darkest moments of her life. It's my voice and no one can hear it unless I want them to.

Now, suddenly, at age thirty, Nora Jane was getting excited about meeting this teacher. I might really be excited about the baby, she tried to tell herself, but she knew it wasn't so. No, the baby is just there. This is because the great feminist writer Adrien Searle is coming to get me and take me to meet Delaney Hawk. Maybe I'll audition for her. Maybe she knew about Grandmother. I bet she knew of her.

What if I really started singing, she was thinking. I would have a concert one day and Freddy and Lydia and Tammili would come and be surprised. They'd say, I don't believe that's our mother.

Navin dressed in blue jeans and a white shirt. He put on a baseball cap to hide his black curls and then added a tweed jacket someone had found for him in a secondhand clothing store. He changed into the new basketball shoes. He put on his flesh-colored gloves. He picked up a knife and held it for a second, then slipped it into his jacket pocket. A small revolver was already taped to his ribs. The marble-sized smoke bombs and explosive devices were in his sleeves. "I will leave the message in the hotel room," he had told Amir. "The closer to home, the more it frightens them. The knife is for the clothes, he told himself, looking into the mirror. Unless better meat presents itself. Amir is too cautious. He has become soft from his time here. He thinks they have power to stop us. He is a bad leader. Then I must lead myself, with Allah's blessing. I must assure my path to heaven, or else perhaps I will be sent home soon. It is in your hands, blessed one, guide me. I am a faithful servant if you show the way.

He went outside and waited for the car to pull up to the curb. A young man named Ali Fava was in the driver's seat. They embraced, then sat back and were quiet. Ali Fava drove him to the Paris Hotel. He got out of the car and went into the hotel through the adjoining coffee shop. He nodded to the man at the desk but did not stop to speak. He got into the elevator and went up to the second floor and found the door to the room and disabled the latch with a wire and let himself into the double room. It was all so quick, so perfect, that if Sebranek and Adrien had been standing by the door they would not have heard it or been able to stop it.

Adrien was in the bathroom. She was dressed and was putting on powder and lipstick. She had meant to spend a long time on her makeup but had been caught up on the phone with an editor at *Harper's Bazaar* and thought she was running out of time. She wanted to talk to Delaney once more before she brought Nora Jane out there. She wanted to stress the importance of not scaring the young woman. Delaney sometimes terrified the young. "She's a special young woman, I will say. From a wealthy and powerful family. Even you need connections, Delaney. So give her a chance. For the sake of our friendship. I've never asked a favor of you, have I?" Adrien practiced the speech, then chided herself for preparing a speech to give to a friend. "Nonsense," she concluded. "I'll just tell her what I want."

She heard the door close. "Sebranek?" she called over her shoulder, still looking in the mirror. "What are you doing back here?" She saw in the mirror the reflection of Navin's face. Like a terrible dream, the beard, the eyes, the knife. Then he was directly behind her and grabbed her head and held her. He stuck the knife into her breast three times. Then he slashed her throat. He was very fastidious and did not like to be bloodied. He let the body drop, then stepped gingerly over her and went to the tub to wash the blood off his gloves. He used a towel to clean his shoes.

He went back into the room and found a plastic bag in a trash can and stuffed the towel into it. He let himself out of the room. He took off the gloves and added them to the bag. Then he went down the back stairs and out onto the patio and through a gate and found Ali Fava waiting with the motor running. He got into the car and threw the bag in the backseat. "Go to the coffeehouse on the corner," he said. "The Peet's. I want to get a pound of coffee. Do as I say. Drive slowly. Roll the windows down. There is no hurry. There is nothing to fear."

"Did you leave a good message?"

"It became complicated. I had to do more than was anticipated. It is unfortunate, but Allah knows all, sees all, directs us. We are servants and must not complain."

"What's in the sack?"

"We'll get rid of it later. Park in front of the coffee shop. You'll go in with me."

Ali Fava did as he was told. He feared Navin. When Navin was in a dark mood, it was unwise to anger him.

At twelve Nora Jane started getting dressed. At one she got into the convertible and drove down the steep driveway and out onto Archer Street, which curves along the bay. The blue-green water and the Golden Gate Bridge were lovely in the hazy noon light. Above the bridge long cumulus clouds moved and gathered, hovering over the bay like angels, waiting for a wind to blow them to the shore.

Nora Jane was sitting up very tall, letting the wind blow her hair. I'm going to meet Delaney Hawk, she was thinking. I might be getting ready to have a career just when I have this baby. Who cares? I can do two or three things at once. It's a new world. I'd never neglect my children. Grandmother used to take Daddy when she'd tour and he grew up to go to Annapolis. I can feel him in me even if I never knew him, even if he did get blown to smithereens in a stupid war. I've got him in me and Grandmother too. I wish she was here today. I was lost and now I'm finding every part of me, that's how I feel today.

She took the ramp off the bridge and went down a side street, then turned onto an avenue. Groups of people were strolling along, shopping, standing on corners, walking dogs. Farther down, in the neighborhood of the hotel where Adrien and

Sebranek were staying, the people seemed older, old hippies and retired rich people, chic little flower shops and coffee shops, art galleries and shoe stores that sold outrageously expensive shoes.

As she neared the hotel she saw police cars blocking the street. Even then I didn't know what it was, she always said later. I didn't have a clue. So if I'm intuitive it sure wasn't turned on that day.

She parked the car and began to walk in the direction of the hotel. I remember hurrying, she would say later. I started walking as fast as I could walk.

As she approached the small front door of the hotel, she saw four orderlies carrying a covered body on a stretcher. Police were everywhere. The people in the adjacent restaurant were lined up at the bar. Their faces were taut and strained. A tear had been made in the fabric of civilized life. Not down in the projects or poor sections of town, but right here, in Berkeley, near Chez Panisse and Black Oak Books, here, where civilization and peace had been worshiped as gods.

"It's a woman," Nora Jane heard someone say. "It's some woman writer."

A policeman was helping the orderlies load the body into an ambulance. Then the doors were shut and the ambulance driver got into the front seat and drove slowly off.

Nora Jane stood for a long moment trying to catch her breath. Then she broke through the crowd and found a policeman and took his sleeve. "Who was it? I was coming here to meet Adrien Searle. Tell me that wasn't who that was on the stretcher."

"That's who it was, lady. Could we have your name? Were you related to Ms. Searle?"

"I was coming to pick her up. She came to do a book party for my husband yesterday. That's why she was here. Where's Sebranek Conrad? Please tell me what happened, what's going on here?"

"Come with me." The policeman led her underneath the wire. He motioned to another officer to take his place, then he led Nora Jane into the hotel. They went past the desk and into a small room where the San Francisco District Attorney's Office had set up a temporary station. "Here's a lady who was coming to pick up the victim," the policeman said, handing her over to a man who seemed to be in charge.

"I'm sorry you walked into this," the man said. "Please sit down. Tell us what you know." He was a nice-looking man with thick strong arms and shoulders that were bulging out of the lightweight fabric of his summer suit. He reminded Nora Jane of the Cajun men in South Louisiana.

"I don't even know what happened. Adrien died? She died here? She was killed?"

"She was stabbed to death. Tell me your name."

"I'm Nora Harwood. My husband owns Clara Books. Ms. Searle came out here to do a reading yesterday. She's the one who wrote that book about the environment that started a congressional investigation. She wrote *End of All Springs*. That was the book, and lots of other books. She changed people's lives. How could she die? Someone killed her?"

"Yes." He waited, as though expecting her to confess.

"I'm pregnant. I just found out. I shouldn't be here like this. Where is Sebranek Conrad? He was with her. I need to call my husband and tell him about this. May I use the phone?"

"Your husband is the reason she came to San Francisco?"

"No, her book is the reason. Sebranek Conrad is her editor. He was with her. Where is he? I need to use the phone, please. What is your name?"

"Jason Hebert. Look, you give me the number. I'll call your husband." She told him the number and he dialed it. He hasn't answered a single one of my questions, Nora Jane was thinking.

"Hebert is a Louisiana name. I'm from New Orleans."

"My folks are from Boutte. I thought I recognized that accent of yours. Wait a minute." He spoke to someone on the phone, then turned back to her. "Get Mrs. Harwood some water, Jake. Sit down, honey. Sit down and drink that water, will you?" He smiled at her then, a sweet smile. He had eyes so brown and kind and worried that Nora Jane settled down beneath their gaze. Then he turned back to the phone. She could only half hear the conversation he was having with Freddy.

She looked down at the glass of water the man named Jake had given her. This isn't true, she decided, this is not happening. That was not Adrien being put into that ambulance. I don't want it to be anyone. Not anyone at all.

Jason Hebert turned back to her. "Your husband's on his way. I wish you'd drink that water. I don't want a miscarriage on top of a murder this afternoon."

"I'd like some bottled water. I can't drink this. The glass doesn't even look clean. Tell me what happened, please."

"Your friend was stabbed to death sometime this morning and was found about eleven-forty-five by the maid, who let herself into the room to clean. That's all we know. It was quick and clean and she didn't put up a fight. Does that help?"

"No, that's horrible. It's terrible. I'm not even sure it's true. How do you know it was her? It might not have been Adrien. It might be someone else was in her room."

He got up and came around the makeshift desk to her chair and took her arm. "Go get some bottled water out of the bar, Jake," he said. "And bring a clean glass." Nora Jane looked up and met those eyes again, extraordinary eyes. The eyes of an altar boy, a darkened church on Poydras or Melepomene. Incense, the mass being read in Latin, death and the smell of death. "You okay?" he asked.

"No, no, I'm not okay at all." Then she began to cry and he reached in his pocket and took out a white handkerchief and handed it to her.

"Can you help us at all?" he asked, when the tears had subsided and she looked at him again. "Tell us who might have done this. Anything you know. Any enemies she had."

"Who knows. Anyone can hate a writer who writes the truth about the world. Anyone can fixate on a writer or stalk them or think they own them because they read their books. Things like that happen. But I never met Adrien Searle until yesterday. She wasn't someone who made enemies. She was this very sweet older lady who was like a mother to everyone. She wasn't someone who gets killed out of hate. Maybe it was a robbery. Did they steal things?"

"Not that we noticed. She had on a watch and rings, and her pocketbook wasn't touched."

"I don't know. Let me think." Nora Jane was crying again. At the thought of the day that had begun so brilliantly and now had ended like this. This was like her childhood had been, fear and anger and uncertainty. Evil that seemed to come from nowhere and darken the sun. One moment her mother would be sober and trying to get in good with her. The next moment she was crying and begging for help and saying she was going to die. Then I went to Grandmother, Nora Jane remembered. I'd walk over there day or night even when I was so little. I'd walk across Magazine Street by myself at night when I was seven years old. I still don't know why I never got run over.

Then Freddy was there, having parked his car on the street behind the police barricade. "I left my automobile on the street," he told Jason Hebert. "See if you can keep them from towing it. It's a dark blue Honda. Are you all right?" He turned to Nora Jane.

"I don't know. I saw them carrying her out. Where is Sebranek?"

"Mr. Conrad is upstairs with our physician," Jason answered. It was as though he had decided it was all right to answer her questions now that Freddy was here. "He's in shock. He returned after we got here. He identified the body. What do you know about his son Johnnie? Do you know where he lives?"

"What does Johnnie have to do with it?" Freddy asked.

"We don't know," Jason answered. "But we need to talk to him. Do you know where he lives?"

"No. He comes in the store occasionally but I don't think he lives in this part of town. Ask Sebranek. He knows where he is."

"We have asked him. I need the two of you to come down to the station and give us a statement sometime today."

"Johnnie Conrad's not involved in this." Freddy stood up very close to Jason and looked him in the eye. "Don't go running down blind alleys while the murderer gets away. I promise you,

Johnnie Conrad wouldn't kill anyone. He probably doesn't even eat meat. What are you people thinking?"

"Two people saw a young man fitting his description hurrying through the lobby at eleven o'clock. They noticed him because he was in such a hurry. He showed up yesterday at her reading, didn't he?"

"How did you know that? Where are you getting all this information? Johnnie Conrad wouldn't have any reason to kill Adrien Searle."

"She broke up his parents' marriage, didn't she?" It became very quiet in the room. Nora Jane stood up and went to Freddy. A chill went through her. They weren't kidding. This wasn't a television movie. They thought Sebranek's son was involved in this.

A detective entered the room. "We found the Conrad kid," he said. "He's running some kind of after-school program down in Soweto. They took him downtown."

"I want to see Sebranek," Freddy said. "You can't be holding him. He needs us. Take us to him before I start calling lawyers, and that's not an idle threat."

"No need for that. I'm sorry this has been so bad for your wife. Jake, go see if Mr. Conrad can come down here. We'll wrap this up and seal off the room and then we'll get downtown. I wish we hadn't walked on that hall carpet. Roll it up and bring it down."

"I took it up an hour ago. You didn't notice?"

"Good. Start talking, Mr. Harwood. Tell me what you know."

"She had enemies. Every anti-environmental person in the West thinks she's the Antichrist. Also, Sebranek publishes Salman Rushdie. Did anyone tell you that? They both surf the edge. It could be anyone, it could be random violence. What it isn't, is anything to do with Sebranek Conrad's son, who graduated, I'm pretty sure of this, summa cum laude from Cornell. That divorce is old, old stuff. Where did you get the idea that the boy they saw in the hall was Johnnie Conrad? What have you been smoking?"

Freddy was getting mad, a dangerous thing. He was the only

son of an extremely wealthy woman who had indulged his every wish since the day he was born. He had firms of lawyers at his beck and call. A detective from the San Francisco police department was nothing to him. Ninety-nine percent of the time he went about his life as if he were an ordinary person. He cultivated wearing old clothes and never letting anyone see his power, but when the one-quarter Irish blood his mother had bequeathed him rose to the top, he boiled. Nora Jane had not seen it often but she had seen it enough to be frightened by it. For all she knew Freddy might haul off and hit Jason Hebert and then they'd both go to jail.

"Oh, please," she said. "This is not the time for this. Please, Freddy, settle down. We have to talk to Sebranek. Think how he's feeling."

"The maid knew Johnnie," Jason said. "She used to be his girlfriend."

Then Sebranek was there and they surrounded him and embraced him and tried to find a way to comfort him but there was no comfort. "Come home with us," Freddy pleaded. "Come to our house."

"I have to go downtown and see about Johnnie. They saw him here. Of course it's some coincidence, but we have to straighten it out." Sebranek pushed them away. He turned to Jason. "Have they found my son?"

"He's on his way downtown. We'll take you with us. Jake, did you see about Mr. Harwood's car?"

"It's right where he left it. Jim's with it."

They went out onto the street and found Freddy's car. "Let me drive you," Freddy said to Nora Jane.

"No, I don't want to leave the car. I'll follow you."

"I don't want you out of my sight."

"I have to take my car home, Freddy. It might get towed."

They stood in the middle of the police barricade, a uniformed policeman holding the car door open. "This is like Vonnegut's description of space travelers looking down on the earth and thinking the inhabitants are little steel automobiles being served by four-limbed bits of protoplasm. Leave the goddamn car there, Nora Jane. We'll send somebody for it."

"I can drive it. I'm better than you are. At least I didn't threaten a detective."

"I'm going to sue some detectives. That was the most inhumane little meeting of minds I've yet encountered. This woman, his love, is dead, murdered, and they're treating him like a suspect."

"Why would Johnnie have been there?"

"I don't know. But we'll find out, won't we." He let her go then and she got into her car and drove slowly home and he followed her. Once or twice he turned on the radio to see if it had made the news but all he could get was music and an update on the weather.

Two hours later Freddy and Nora Jane and Freddy's best friend, Nieman, and Freddy's bookkeeper, Frances, were in the Harwood living room manning phones. The media had the story now and were playing it for all it was worth. It had been a godsend to the media. There was no foreign news of interest to the citizens of the United States and no new scandals in Washington. What scandals there were concerned money and banks and bond fraud. Americans are too healthy to stay interested for long in theft. Murder and passion and revenge are what the American public likes on a nice spring day, and Adrien Searle's death promised all that and more.

Nieman and Freddy were doing what they could to control the damage. They were calling in their chits with reporters all over the country. The *San Francisco Chronicle,* the *Los Angeles Times,* the *New York Times,* the *Boston Globe,* CNN, the Associated Press, the United Press. All three phones were ringing without stop as reporters they knew called back and forth gathering parts of the story. Johnnie was being held for questioning and the media had gotten hold of the Conrads' divorce and Johnnie's years of therapy and Sebranek's ex-wife's crippling arthritis and her brother's unsuccessful Senate race and Sebranek's rise to literary fame and the Rushdie connection.

"Take a break," Freddy said at dusk. "Turn the phones off and let's eat something. Where are the girls, Nora Jane?"

"They're here. They're fine." She pulled the master phone plug out of the wall and the four friends turned to face each other on the white chairs Freddy had bought when he was in his Scandinavian mood.

"They'll have Adrien's sons in it by night," Nieman was saying. "Didn't you tell me she doesn't talk to one of them? That's pathological enough to occupy a day's news, wouldn't you say? This is turning into a mess, a real mess."

"It's already a mess. Adrien's dead." Nora Jane got up and took Nieman's glass to fill it. He was drinking wine.

"'Things fall apart,'" Freddy quoted, "'the center cannot hold. . . . The best lack all conviction while the worst are full of passionate intensity.' Yeats. This is the tip of the iceberg, Nieman. You and I know Johnnie didn't kill Adrien, and in the meantime whoever did is running the streets of San Francisco. I'm thinking of sending Nora Jane and the girls down to the Baja to Mother's place."

"You are not sending me anywhere. What is it, darling?" Tammili had come to stand in the door.

"May I use the phone now? Tara thinks I'm going to call her. She's going to get mad at me and we just made up. If I don't call her she's going to get mad again."

"Of course you may call her. Come over here. What's that in your hair?"

"Lydia's making dreadlocks. She made me one."

"Come here to me, goddaughter of my heart." Nieman held out his hands to her. "A friend died, Tammili. But it will never touch you in any way. We are calling reporters so they won't write foolishness in their newspapers. We are trying to maintain civilization and that is why the phones have been busy. What's this about your friend Tara? Your friendship is in danger, fraught with people getting mad?"

"Don't laugh at me," she said, but she went to him and let him hug her and he plugged in a phone and helped her dial her friend, having to cut out incoming signals as they dialed.

"She wants me to come over," Tammili said, when she had

hung up the phone. "It's not dark yet. May I ride my bike to her house?"

"Go on then," Nora Jane said. "Tell Lydia to come in here and let me see what she's doing to her hair. Never mind, I'll go in there. Did Betty give you supper? Did you eat supper?"

"Yes."

"Well, go to Tara's until eight o'clock. Then come right back."

"I'll take her," Freddy said. He got up and put down the papers he was holding.

"It's only four houses. Leave her alone. We can't change their lives. Go on, honey. She and Tara are doing a science project. They have to work on it."

Tammili left the room and Freddy followed her. She went to the carport and found her bicycle and wheeled it out onto the long driveway that curved down the acre of land to the street.

Freddy stood by the front steps watching her. Two of his three sheepdogs ran over and begged to be petted. He caressed their fine big heads. An old male named Prospero and his grand-daughter, a high-strung beauty they called Cleo. It was growing dark. To the west there was a cloud bank of unearthly blue, so subtle and evanescent that it changed as Freddy watched. Cleo nuzzled his hand. Prospero pushed her away and stood against his leg like a pillar.

Tammili's bike moved down the long drive and out onto the sidewalk and continued down the hill. As she passed a hedge of azalea bushes, a man rose up and stood in her way. Tammili screamed. Freddy and the dogs began to run. The dogs were there before the bicycle finished falling. Then Tammili was on the ground with a dog on top of her and the man was running down the street with the second dog pursuing. He jumped into an old red car and drove away.

Cleo returned to Freddy. She was holding a piece of torn leather in her mouth. She was slobbering and breathing hard when Freddy reached her but would not let go of the leather.

Prospero was with Tammili, licking her and whining. He was making little short breathy whines. Tammili was petting him as she extricated her legs from the bike. She stood up in a rage. "He hit Prospero with a gun," she said. "He hit him on the back.

Poor old Prospero, poor old wonderful dog." She was examining the animal for wounds. Freddy bent over to look for cuts on her legs.

Nora Jane and Nieman were running down the yard with Lydia behind them. "Call the police," Freddy yelled to them. "Call the neighborhood patrol."

Fifteen minutes later a bomb went off in the front window of Clara Books. It destroyed an exhibit of first editions of Karsh and Ansel Adams monographs and took out the entire travel and poetry sections. There were books there that would never be in print again. All the Lost Roads and Dragonseed editions printed on paper made to last a thousand years. All the Faber and Faber hardbacks. It would be a long time before the extent of the damage was fully revealed to the staff of Clara Books, the oldest and least economically successful privately owned bookstore in the Bay Area. But that is a different tragedy. "And furnished me with books from my own library, which I prize above my dukedom," as the real Prospero said.

The neighborhood patrol beat the police to the house. Jason Hebert was right behind them. He had been on his way to tell Freddy about the bombing. Before he reached the door he got news of Tammili's assailant.

"We assume this is all related until we find a reason not to believe it," he said. "I'm really sorry about your store. We have it cordoned off. I'll take you down there if you want to go."

"I have a piece of the jacket," Freddy answered. "I had a time getting it from the dog but I tried not to touch it. I wrapped it in plastic. What do you want me to do with it?"

"Your family will be under our protection," Jason answered. "It will be a twenty-four-hour watch. I want you to know they will be safe."

"You're leaving in the morning and taking the girls with you." Freddy was folding his clothes to leave on the chair overnight. It was a habit he had gotten into at Exeter and he always fell back into it when he was thinking. No matter how wrinkled or dirty the clothes were, if Freddy was thinking hard he folded each piece as he took it off and stacked the pieces on a chair. He took his socks off next to last and his underpants off right before he got into bed. He was taking his socks off now. As he rolled them into a neat roll, Nora Jane knew she was in for it.

"You can go to Mother's house or up to Willits or to Europe. If the house on the beach was finished you could go there. What you can't do is stay in this house with my children and my unborn child until we find out what's going on."

"We are perfectly safe. The police are watching us. Nothing is going to harm us here. I'm not leaving, Freddy. It would scare the girls to death. I don't think that man was after Tammili. It was some sort of coincidence. Besides, I won't be run out of my own house by murderers. I want to go see Mrs. Hawk and ask her what Adrien said to her on the phone. I told Inspector Hebert I was going to help."

"Help! What are you talking about? You don't help in a murder investigation. Good Lord, Nora Jane. I don't believe you said that. This has nothing to do with you."

"It does have to do with me. I liked Adrien so much. Oh, God, do you think she knew they were going to kill her? Do you think she had time to think?"

"You're in denial. They bombed the store. A man was in our azalea bushes. And, yes, she had time, they slit her throat, which is why you're leaving here."

"Come get in bed. I'm scared too, Freddy. But I'm not leaving unless you do. I'd be more scared being away from you than being here." She patted the pillow, tried to pretend to look seductive, but it didn't work.

"I'm going to look in on the girls first."

"Nieman's sleeping in the room next to them with the door open. And you know he never sleeps."

"I'll just look." Freddy padded down the hall barefooted and looked in on the girls. Then he looked in at Nieman, lying on his back in the guest room pretending to be asleep.

Freddy returned to his bed and got in beside his wife. "Can you believe he insisted on staying here? That's just like him. I love Nieman, Nora Jane. He's a pillar. He's never let me down."

"Go to sleep," Nora Jane said. "Come here to me. This is our house. No one can harm us here."

Night settles down upon this house, Nieman was thinking. Night fills the oceans and the valleys and the towns, night falls on this murderer, this sick or benighted person whom it serves no purpose to hate or fear. Only reason can save us now, and reason is slow, so slow. Reason is the turtle in the race, and reason demands that I sleep. I will sleep. Nieman relaxed the muscles in his cerebral cortex, he relaxed the muscles that pump blood to the brain, he relaxed the muscles that control the eyes. He set his sights on Athena and he slept. He was not always this fortunate in controlling his brain's whims.

As soon as they finished breakfast the next morning, Nieman and Freddy went into a small office behind the kitchen to decide how to proceed. It had been a maid's room when Freddy bought the house. Later he had turned it into a reading room. The walls were lined with the books he had owned when he was a student. The sofa was covered with an old blanket he had taken to camp as a child. He sat down upon it now and it seemed to give him strength.

Nieman sat facing him. "Don't talk," he said. "Think."

"Figure out who the enemy is. Who would kill Adrien, then bomb my store. If it was Muslim fundamentalists they would have announced themselves, wouldn't they? Isn't that how they operate?"

"Look for the thing we have forgotten. Is there a money trail? Is it about you or Nora Jane? Someone who works for the store?"

"No. No way."

"Is it Sebranek?"

"It looks that way. But then, if they are after Sebranek, why bomb the store? It would hurt him more if suspicion stayed on Johnnie."

"Are the two things related? That's the real question."

"And what of the man who startled Tammili? That's the thing that's driving me crazy. Right here, in my yard, on my property, while I watched. If the bombing is related to that, we have to leave San Francisco. The house on the beach will be finished in a month. It might be safe there. At least the property is open and could be watched. God, Nieman, is this happening to us? What effect will it have on the girls?"

"I was up half the night pondering that one."

"Tammili's spooked, whether she admits it or not. She's probably listening outside the door right now. Nora Jane kept them home from school." Freddy got up and went to the door and opened it. The only sound was the dishwasher in the kitchen.

"Is it about our being Jews?"

"I don't know." They were silent. Then Nieman raised his arms as though to conduct a symphony.

"Freddy, why didn't we think of it? There's the new Center for Middle Eastern Studies at Berkeley. I met the director the other day. I'd been so derisive and irritated about it and then I ran into the director in Musa's office and he turned out to be rather nice. Affable, trying to make friends. He's a Palestinian Christian, a Doctor Zouabi, something like that. I was struggling so hard to overcome my prejudices so we could talk that I didn't get his name. Let's go over there and get him to give us a reading on it. We can't rely on the police, or even the FBI on this one. We have to make our own assessment. Don't you agree?"

"Call him now. Make an appointment." Freddy got up quietly and pulled open the door and caught sight of Tammili's red shirt disappearing around a corner.

Three hours later they were sitting in a crowded cubicle in the old administration building, part of which had been turned into the new Center for Middle Eastern Studies. Freddy and Nieman told Doctor Zouabi what they knew, including the Salman Rushdie problems of the past.

"Who do you think is after us and why?" Freddy asked. "I want to meet them and talk to them. I'll take his books out of the store if it's still Salman. I mean it. Find out what they want."

"Can you help us?" Nieman added. "Can you find out anything?"

"I can try. I'm more suspect by those factions than you are. They are not happy about our work here."

"Do you have an idea?"

"There are hit lists. Perhaps your Mr. Sebranek Conrad is on one of them." He laced his fingers together. He was an extraordinarily ugly man, wearing very expensive corduroy trousers and fine leather shoes with cashmere socks. A silk shirt, a dark green alpaca sweater. A gold watch. There were rings.

He's got about twelve grand on his person, Freddy decided. Then bowed his head. Don't be prejudiced, he warned himself. You have come for help. Don't project prejudice or hate. Help me, you son-of-a-bitch. Tell me which of your ugly benighted countrymen is after my life and my children.

"If you get information for me I'll make a grant to your foundation in gratefulness," Freddy said. "If they want Salman's books out of the store they can have that." I'm sick of fighting this battle. I don't have to defend free speech for Muslims who don't believe in it anyway. To hell with it. I should have given up when they bombed me last time.

"He's overwrought," Nieman added. "As you can see. We appreciate your seeing us. We're grateful to you already." If you want to veil your women and keep harems, go on with it, he was thinking. But then, you're a Christian, aren't you? So the university believes, anyway. Well, I won't be prejudiced. I'll outgrow my conditioning. I'll rise above it. I swear I will but not today in all probability, not with you wearing those pants and that watch and those rings.

When they were gone, Doctor Hava Zouabi picked up the phone and began to call numbers on two continents. At six o'clock that night he got what he wanted. "Two Jews are being harassed over some book-selling Jew from New York City," he said. "They want to apologize and buy someone off. Do you know who might want an apology from a bookstore in San Francisco?" He listened for a while, then wrote down a name and an address. "Thank you, Saleem, God be with you."

It's good when they learn a lesson, he decided. How much I hate this ugly place, these ugly big people and their heartiness and disdain. Three more years. I will suffer it and cause my little children to suffer it for three more years, then I will go home. I will never set foot in their filthy cities again. Never watch their piglike children slop around the streets all day and night, their whores of women, their television sets.

He closed up his little cubicle and walked the seven blocks to his rented house and went inside and kissed his children and let his wife bathe and feed him and put him to sleep for the night.

III

"We must grow or die," Freddy said, when they were in the car with Nieman driving. "We have read Amos Oz. We have seen the bodies of our children and their children. If this is about Salman, the books go out of the store. I won't put my family in jeopardy for him. Let him apologize to his people or take the stupid book out of print. Who cares? If you think for one moment I'm not serious about this, you're wrong. I hate them. It's true, deep down inside where I can never root it out I hate and fear them and wish them dead. I cannot rise above this, Nieman. There must be a way to ride above it then. A way to constantly know how stupid it is. Hate and war make hate and war. They destroy the reasons men attain the property over which they fight. The idea is to protect women and children and then the women and children end up being killed." Freddy rolled his shoulders into a ball as he spoke. He curled his body into itself. He undid his seat belt so he could think better. His hair was very thick and curly and he was nearly always in need of a haircut. Today it was even dirty.

"You look like an Arab street kid with that hair. Let me put it this way. If you remove Salman's books from the store and apologize to the Arab world it's all right with me. As long as that's the enemy in this case and I'm not sure it is. I'm not blameless in this hatred and you know it. Just because I try to be rational doesn't mean my mother wasn't just as big a bigot and ball- and soul-breaker as yours was. They all are. That's what they do and we must forgive them every morning and move on.

"Freddy, I woke up this morning thinking about what was in the window of the store the day they bombed it. It doesn't make sense. Ansel Adams photographs Then I started thinking. You put that exhibit up the day after Adrien spoke. I was by there the day before she spoke to buy a book about coins for my nephew and the front window was a mess. There were displays of Adrien's books and photographs of her. But that was crowded into a small space. All around it were piles of mess. I was meaning to say something to you about it. I thought it was disrespectful to have her things all crowded in with everyone else's pet agendas. Every rabid feminist of the last ten years was represented, as though Adrien was not a law unto herself with broad-ranging interests. What was all that stuff?"

"Nieman, stop the car. Do you realize what you just said? That was a pro-choice display from the day before. I guess Frances just crowded it to the back to put Adrien's books in the window. The women had a benefit for Planned Parenthood the day before Adrien came. One of the speakers was that Palestinian woman they're all so crazy about who says all men are rapists. What if it was unrelated? What if Adrien's death had nothing to do with the bombing? All these years I pay lip service to the scientific method and when I need it, what do I do? Jump to the first conclusion that occurs to me. Tammili keeps saying the license plate on the car said Alabama. She reads all the mysteries she can get her hands on. She would read a license plate, wouldn't she? We would have when we were her age. Don't stop the car. Go down to Jason Hebert's office and let's talk to him."

"I wasn't going to stop the car. We're on the freeway, Freddy. I thought you wanted to go see about the store."

"Frances will take care of the store. Go to Jason's office now."

Doctor Hava Zouabi was still worrying about the visit Freddy and Nieman had paid to him. He picked up the phone and began to call numbers he should not have been calling from his office phone. He called the cell in New York City and the one in Los Angeles and the man in Los Alamos. "They said Amir might know why a bookstore was bombed and a woman killed," he asked these people.

"Amir is not interested in bookstores," they answered him.

"Is he interested in Salman Rushdie?"

"No one bothers with Salman Rushdie now. Let him stew in his own juice. He has angered the British. He has been ungrateful and the British don't like that. We have other mares to tame, Doctor Zouabi. Don't be involved in things that don't interest you. Do your work. Trust in Allah. Allah be praised."

"Life is good. Allah be praised."

Lydia and Tammili and Nora Jane and two detectives were in the Harwoods' living room. Tammili and Lydia were wearing matching navy blue jumpers and white blouses. They were wearing the gold bracelets they had gotten for their tenth birthday. They were wearing white tennis shoes and new white Nike socks. Lydia had her hand on Tammili's arm.

"It said ALA 540, then I couldn't see the rest," Tammili was saying. "It wasn't dark and I wasn't really hurt and Prospero was on top of me but I could see. I have twenty-twenty vision. The first thing I did was look at the license plate. It said ALA 540. He was as skinny as he could be and he had on that black jacket and Cleopatra tore off a piece of it. How did those dogs know what to do? That's what I want to know. Did they read my mind or did they know he was mean?" She sat up very straight. Tammili wasn't afraid. She lived in the center of a group of people who would kill or die or move to Malibu for her. What did she have to fear?

"Could it have said AR?" the detective asked. "Think very hard, Tammili. Think as hard as you can."

"It might have. There was an A and the plate was white with dark letters. I thought it was ALA but if you put the 5 very close to the A I guess it could. It could. I'll say provisionally it could." *Provisionally* was one of the vocabulary words Nieman had sent her last week on E-mail. She had been looking for a way to use it.

"Then we may be on to something. There's an antiabortion ring we've been watching who have a dark red Chevrolet with Arkansas plates. It's a stolen car. We've been letting them keep it because it makes it easy to track them. Stolen from a used car lot in Fort Smith, Arkansas. One of their favorite targets lately is bookstores. They stole all the feminist books out of a big discount store in L.A. We've been waiting for them to do something we can jail them for. We found the jacket, by the way. It was thrown away several blocks from here. A cheap leather jacket made in Taiwan like ones that are sold in jeans stores everywhere."

"Then it has nothing to do with Adrien's murder, does it?" Nora Jane shook her head from side to side as she spoke. She was becoming terrified at last. "What does any of this mean? If these people scared Tammili and bombed our store, why did they do it? I don't get it. None of it makes sense. Is there anything else you need Tammili to tell you?"

"Not unless she can remember something she didn't tell us yesterday." The detective folded his hands. They were good hands, wide and strong and freckled. Another altar boy, Nora Jane decided, I cannot escape them anywhere. The Church. Its shadows are everywhere. Light and shadow, that's all we know. The past, the past, the past. She saw herself going with her mother into the darkened sanctuary, her mother smelling of whiskey and cigarettes. She would have been better if she'd gone to AA meetings, Nora Jane decided, but then, they have AA meetings at churches, don't they? Good and bad, in constant battle for the world. The goddamn antiabortionists, the fools. And yet, they call it into play. They force the issue, don't they? I didn't abort the girls and God knows, there was no reason to have them. I didn't even know who they belonged to. Still am not sure. Of course we know. We know. Tammili is Freddy's and Lydia belongs to Sandy and I fucked two men in two days and got pregnant like an alley cat. And that's the past and I've been shriven for that a million times for sure.

"What are you thinking?" the detective asked.

"Are you a Roman Catholic?"

"I was."

"Me too. Those groups make you think about it. They may be crazy but it works. It gets our attention."

"If they bombed our store they should be put in prison for the rest of their lives," Tammili said. "They are trampling on our First Amendment rights."

"Who told you that?"

"Uncle Nieman."

"Are you finished?" Nora Jane stood up. The detective met her eye. Realms of discourse passed between them. Nora Jane was especially beautiful this day, with her high cheekbones and wide green eyes and her passion and her fear. She was lovelier now than she had been when she was younger. Lovelier than the night she met Freddy Harwood, when she tried to rob him with a wooden gun and ended up talking to him all night and crying in his arms. Freddy could never remember what they said that night. I am a creature of language, he had told Nieman later. But all I can remember is her face and the way she moved her hands when she spoke. There are Graces, I decided. And they have chosen this woman as their proof.

Now the poor twenty-nine-year-old detective from the San Francisco Police Department was suffering that face and that voice and those graces. He stood up beside her and tried not to let it show.

"That's all," he said. "The D.A. just wanted us to see if there was a chance we'd got it right about the car."

Nora Jane turned to her children. "You all go find something to do for a while. Your grandmother wants to take you shopping later. Did I tell you that? Do you want to go with her?"

"Yes." They looked at each other and giggled. They loved going shopping with their grandmother. Nora Jane and Freddy were contemptuous of malls but their grandmother Ann approached a mall as if it were a carnival. She had even let them ride a centrifugal-force machine.

"Then go on and call and tell her you're ready." Nora Jane watched them leave the room, then moved closer to the detective. "Tell me more about this group of people from Arkansas."

"Actually, they're from Utah. They have a stolen car with Arkansas plates. They're dangerous people. If we could pin this bombing on them, it would be a help."

"I think it's about Salman Rushdie. I don't think it's about Mormon sects. They wouldn't bother to come to where our store is. They wouldn't even know about that part of Berkeley."

"Nuts are everywhere."

"Then where is it safe to live?"

"Not in this city," he answered. "If you knew what I know you couldn't sleep at night."

In the Los Angeles office of the Muslim fundamentalist group to which Doctor Hava Zouabi was attached as a spy and a terrified tool, they had called a meeting to discuss the telephone conversations he had been making in the last few days. "He's beginning to think he's a free agent," Amir was saying. "The university people have spoiled him. He has forgotten the thirty million dollars our country gave them for their school. He has begun to believe they are interested in what he has to say. I think it's time he went home before he loses his usefulness altogether. He made three phone calls from his office to special numbers. We had all the numbers changed, of course, but it was unthinking. We need a more attractive man in the job. He's not presentable with that pockmarked face. It confirms their prejudices. I was thinking Mostapha might be better in the position."

"How could we explain his leaving?"

"An illness. That's easy enough to arrange."

"What of the bookstore people? Has there been any decision on Salman lately?"

"Let Salman stew in his juice. Public opinion in Britain is turning against him. If anyone gets to him, of course, so much the better."

"Will we claim credit for the bookstore?"

"Childish idea. It was bungled, amateur and messy. Abdel says it was a Christian group from Utah. Of no interest to us."

"What of the emir in New York City? It was his disciple who took the woman in the hotel."

"We will rescue them when the time comes. He's an old man. It's good for people to see they have no pity for him. We have made our point. They know we can reach them. The times of jihad will come. Two shipments from Cologne got through the airport. It all goes as planned. There is much we know. Much we cannot know. Allah be praised."

"Allah be praised."

*   *   *

Jason Hebert was in his office staring at a poster that read CONVICTION IS THE ENEMY OF TRUTH. It was covered with a fine layer of dust and he was thinking of getting up and wiping it off with his handkerchief when Freddy and Nieman were ushered in.

"I'm glad you came," he said. "We think we know who your intruder was. He's part of a Mormon sect that broke off from the Church in Utah. Just another bunch of crazies who went to the hills to have four wives. Only this bunch has a leader who's a real nut. Kid from Salt Lake City whose father left them early. His mother ran a halfway house for unwed mothers. All the babies given up for adoption. A couple of the girls committed suicide later. About the time he was nineteen he left home and started collecting followers. He's a good-looking devil, a natural leader. We're pretty sure it was one of them outside your house. Maybe him. But we don't know why. What could you have done to get the attention of that bunch?"

"That's why we're here," Freddy began. "We had a feminist enclave the day before Adrien spoke. They may have thought she was part of that. Her books were in the same window with all the feminist books. Could they have planted the device and it went off the wrong day? Or did they get Adrien mixed up with someone else? She was a feminist too, but that wasn't the main thrust of her books."

"This crowd isn't smart enough to know the difference, but killing women in hotel rooms isn't part of their m.o. I'd have a hard time fitting that in. I think they're doing peyote. I was around in the seventies. I can spot drug behavior. Each drug leaves a trail for me. I can smell it."

"What would I have done?" Nieman asked.

"Nothing. Bottled water."

"That's right. He had the first filter system in Berkeley. So Adrien could have died for a mistake?" Freddy sat down in the chair facing Jason's desk. "All of it could be a mistake. Just being in the public eye. Even being there can endanger someone's life. That's what we've come to?"

"Technology allowed madness to spread," Nieman said. "And yet, most of us would be dead without it. Bill Clinton is the last president who will ever give a damn about the poor, and his days are limited."

"Where is Sebranek?" Freddy asked. "We can't find him."

"He's with his son. We released the body. They are taking it to New York in the morning."

"We haven't heard from him all day. Then Nieman remembered what was in the window and we decided to come down here. Adrien's books were in the window with everyone a Mormon sect would hate."

"We released a statement apologizing for picking up Johnnie Conrad. It's not sufficient, but it will help."

"Was Johnnie at the hotel?"

"No, the girl changed her story. She went out with him a year ago, once. She went crazy because she saw the body. No one's blaming her for anything. She's in bad shape."

"Many harbor madness waiting for an outlet," Nieman said. He put his hand on Freddy's sleeve. "Let's go home, old friend. I've had enough of this day. We'll go by the museum and look at the jade Buddha and try to stop the madness in our own hearts."

"Is my family safe?" Freddy stood up and faced Jason. Jason shook his head. It took him a moment to answer.

"I feel they are. We'll keep a police watch on you for a while. Until we can round up some of the Holy Rollers and question them. I don't think you were the targets. I think it's broader than that, unspecific."

"That's not an answer."

"I know."

"Thank you for the work you do." Freddy shook his hand and then he and Nieman walked silently back to Nieman's car and got into it and drove away.

"Do you want to stop and see the Buddha?"

"Not today."

"I'm scared."

"So am I, old buddy."

Sebranek was talking to Nora Jane on the phone. "I'm with Johnnie," he said. "They're baking cookies. Where do you buy

a stove? Do you know somewhere that would have a stove
delivered in a hurry?"

"Sure. Call Sears. They're the only ones who service them.
Not that I'm prejudiced."

"I forgot. Freddy's grandmother owned it, didn't she? You
wouldn't have a number, would you?"

"When are you leaving? What's going on?"

"We'll have the service tomorrow in New York. I'm leaving
tonight. Johnnie's going with me. You wouldn't know someone
I could hire to come down here and work until he gets back,
someone who might be good at fixing things and playing basketball?"

"I don't know where you are, Sebranek. Start at the beginning."

"I'm watching Johnnie work. I didn't know he worked. I've
never seen him work. It's a light in the cave. I don't want him
to leave it to go with me but he's insisting."

Which is how it happened that Freddy Harwood and Nieman
Gluuk ended up spending the weekend overseeing the installa-
tion of a stove, a refrigerator, a washer and dryer, and two
portable basketball goals in a warehouse in the heart of the most
dangerous ghetto in San Francisco. Nieman brought along a
young black reporter from the Arts Live section of the *Chronicle*.
"He'll get a story out of it," he excused himself to Freddy. "You
know I don't use people."

Freddy brought Tammili because she insisted on going along.

In New York City, in a church on Fifth Avenue, Sebranek and
Johnnie and half the literary community of the East Coast were
burying Adrien Searle.

The Episcopal priest raised the cup, the organ played "Amazing Grace," there was not a dry eye in the packed church. The
body of Adrien Searle was now either completely irrelevant to
the universe of particles and waves, or else, alive in Sebranek's
brain, or else, what had been Adrien was coiled deep within the
eggs of her five-year-old granddaughter, waiting for some sperm
worth devouring.

*   *   *

In San Francisco Nieman was paying the pizza delivery man for twenty cheese and pepperoni pizzas and Tammili was setting the picnic tables with blue and white paper tablecloths.

The redheaded girl was worrying that Johnnie might never come back and the Sears deliverymen were trying to remember they were being paid time and a half for Saturday work and forget they were in Soweto risking their lives.

The youngest deliveryman finished his work on the refrigerator, then decided, what the hell, he'd do the plumbing for free. "If someone will take me home later," he said to Freddy.

"We'll get you home," Freddy promised. He smiled at the young man and approved of him to the tenth power, something the young man had never gotten at home.

Which is how Milton House came to leave his job at Sears and grow his hair out to his shoulders and spend his mornings getting an M.A. in social work and his afternoons being in love with Johnnie Conrad's girl and having his mind bent by Johnnie's superior mind. But that is another story.

Back at their house Nora Jane and Lydia were having lunch by the pool. They had made pita bread sandwiches filled with sprouts and chopped celery and tomatoes and green peppers. They were drinking iced Sports Tea and talking about perfume and ballet.

"My grandmother would put a drop of perfume on her letters if she wrote to anyone she used to know when she was a diva," Nora Jane was saying. "She didn't have much money by then but she always had that perfume."

"But singing doesn't ruin your feet like ballet does. Maybe Tammili was right to quit. I'm going to quit too. Aurora Morris's big sister had to have her feet operated on because she got these bone spurs and Madame Gautier can barely dance anymore. If I was seventy years old and all I'd been doing was riding my bike I bet I wouldn't be crippled like she is."

"No one cares if you take it or not. You can quit anytime you like."

"What do you want me to do?" Lydia put down her sandwich

and went around the table and put her arms around her mother's neck. "You say."

"I want you to be smart and use your brain and pass math and wear yellow once a week so I can look at you in it." Nora Jane giggled. It was enough. Her child's arms around her neck was sufficient reason to love the earth. The earth was not an evil place. Murder and pain and evil did not rule the earth. Children do, and loving them and watching them and listening to them grow. Amen.

You Must Change
Your Life

In January of nineteen hundred and ninety-five the esteemed movie critic of the *San Francisco Chronicle* took an unapproved leave of absence from his job and went back to Berkeley full time to study biochemistry. He gave his editor ten days' notice, turned in five hastily written, unusually kind reviews of American movies, and walked out.

Why did the feared and admired Nieman Gluuk walk out on a career he had spent twenty years creating? Was it a midlife crisis? Was he ill? Had he fallen in love? The Bay Area arts community forgot about the Simpson trial in its surprise and incredulity.

Let them ponder and search their hearts. The only person who knows the truth is Nieman Gluuk and he can't tell because he can't remember.

The first thing Nieman did after he turned in his notice was call his mother. "I throw up my hands," she said. "This is it, Nieman. The last straw. Of course you will not quit your job."

"I'm going back to school, Mother. I'm twenty years behind in knowledge. I have led the life you planned for me as long as I can lead it. I told you. That's it. I'll call you again on Sunday."

"Don't think I'm going to support you when you're broke,"

she answered. "I watched your father ruin his life following his whims. I swore I'd protect you from that."

"Don't protect me," he begged. "Get down on your knees and pray you won't protect me. I'm forty-four years old. It's time for me to stop pacing in my cage. I keep thinking of the poem by Rilke.

> *"His vision, from the constantly passing bars,*
> *has grown so weary that it cannot hold*
> *anything else. It seems to him there are*
> *a thousand bars; and behind the bars, no world.*
>
> *As he paces in cramped circles, over and over,*
> *the movement of his powerful soft strides*
> *is like a ritual dance around a center*
> *in which a mighty will stands paralyzed.*
>
> *Only at times, the curtain of the pupils*
> *lifts, quietly—An image enters in,*
> *rushes down through the tensed, arrested muscles,*
> *plunges into the heart and is gone."*

"You are not Rilke," his mother said. "Don't dramatize yourself, Nieman. You have a lovely life. The last thing you need is to go back to Berkeley and get some crazy ideas put in your head. This is Freddy Harwood's doing. This has Freddy written all over it."

"Freddy's in it. I'll admit that. He and Nora Jane and I have gone back to school together. I wish I hadn't even called you. I'm hanging up."

"Freddy has a trust fund and you don't. You never remember that, Nieman. Don't expect me to pick up the pieces when this is over. . . ." Nieman had hung up the phone. It was a radical move but one to which he often resorted in his lifelong attempt to escape the woman who had borne him.

Nieman's return to academia had started as a gesture of friendship. Nieman and Freddy had attended Berkeley in the sixties but Nora Jane was fifteen years younger and had never attended college, not even for a day.

"Think how it eats at her," Freddy told him. "We own a bookstore and she never even had freshman English. If anyone asks her where she went to school, she still gets embarrassed. I tell her it's only reading books but she won't believe it. She wants a degree and I want it for her."

"Let's go with her," Nieman said, continuing a conversation they had had at lunch the day before. "I mean it. Ever since she mentioned it I keep wanting to tell her what to take. Last night I decided I should go and take those things myself. We're dinosaurs, Freddy. Our education is outdated. We should go and see what they're teaching."

"Brilliant," Freddy said. "It's a slow time at the store. I could take a few weeks off."

"Here's how I figure it." Nieman stood up, got the bottle of brandy, and refilled their glasses. "We sign up for a few classes, pay the tuition, go a few weeks, and then quit. The university gets the tuition and Nora Jane gets some company until she settles in."

"We have spent vacations doing sillier things," Freddy said, thinking of the year they climbed Annapurna, or the time they took up scuba diving to communicate with dolphins.

"I need a change," Nieman confessed, sinking down into the water until it almost reached his chin. "I'm lonely, Freddy. Except for the two of you I haven't any friends. Everyone I know wants something from me or is angry with me for not adoring their goddamn, whorish movies. Some of them hate me for liking them. It's a web I made and I've caught myself."

"We'll get applications tomorrow. Nora Jane's already registered. Classes start next Monday."

Nieman went to the admissions office the next day and signed up to audit Dante in Translation and Playwriting One. Then, suddenly, after a night filled with dreams, he changed the classes to biochemistry and Introduction to the Electron Microscope.

This was not an unbidden move. For several years Nieman had become increasingly interested in science. He had started by reading books by physicists, especially Freeman Dyson. Physics led to chemistry, which led to biology, which led to him, Nieman Gluuk, a walking history of life on earth. Right there, in every cell in his body was the whole amazing panorama that led to language and conscious thought.

The first lecture on biochemistry and the first hour with the microscopes excited Nieman to such an extent he was trembling when he left the building and walked across the campus to the coffee shop where he had agreed to meet Freddy and Nora Jane. A squirrel climbed around a tree while he was watching. A girl walked by, her hair trailing behind her like a wild tangled net. A bluejay landed on a branch and spread his tailfeathers. Nieman's breath came short. He could barely put one foot in front of the other. Fields of wonder, he said to himself. Dazzling, dazzling, dazzling. If they knew what they are carrying as they go. Time, what a funny word for the one-way street we seem to have to follow.

"This is it," he told Freddy and Nora Jane, when they were seated at a table with coffee and croissants and cream and sugar and butter and jam and honey before them on the handmade plates. "I'm quitting the job. I'm going back to school full time. I have to have this body of information. Proteins and nucleic acids, the chain of being. This is not some sudden madness, Freddy. I've been moving in this direction. I'll apply for grants. I'll be a starving student. Whatever I have to do."

"We don't think you're crazy," Nora Jane said. "We think you're wonderful. I feel like I did this. Like I helped."

"Helped! You are the Angel of the Annunciation is what you are, you darling, you."

"Are you sure this isn't just another search for first causes?" Freddy warned. "Remember those years you wasted on philosophy?"

"Of course it is. So what? This isn't dead philosophical systems or Freudian simplicities. This is real knowledge. Things we can measure and see. Information that allows us to manipulate the physical world."

"If you say so."

"May I borrow the house at Willits for the weekend? I need

to be alone to think. I want to take the textbooks up there and read them from start to finish. I haven't been this excited in years. My God, I am in love."

"Of course you can borrow the house. Just be sure to drain the pipes when you leave."

"It might snow up there this weekend," Nora Jane put in. "The weather station warned of snow."

Two days later Nieman was alone in the solar-powered house Freddy and his friends had built on a dirt road five miles from Willits, California. The house was begun in 1974 and completed in 1983. Many of the boards had been nailed together by Nieman himself with his delicate hands.

The house stood in the center of one hundred and seven acres of land and overlooked a pleasant valley where panthers still hunted. In any direction there was not a power line or telephone pole or chimney. The house had a large open downstairs with a stone bathroom. A ladder led from the kitchen area to a loft with sleeping rooms. There were skylights in the roof and a wall of glass facing east. There was a huge stone fireplace with a wide hearth. Outside there was a patio and a deep well for drinking water. "This well goes down to the center of the earth," Freddy was fond of saying. "We cannot imagine the springs or rivers from which it feeds. This could be water captured eons ago before the crust cooled. This water could be the purest thing you'll ever taste."

"It tastes good," his twin daughters, Tammili and Lydia, would always answer. "It's the best water in the world, I bet."

Nieman stood in the living room looking out across the valleys, which had become covered with snow while he slept. He had arrived late the night before and built up the fire and slept on the hearth in his sleeping bag. "It was the right thing to do to come up here," he said out loud. "This holy place where my friends and I once made our stand against progress and the destruction of the natural world. This holy house where Tammili and Lydia were born, where the panther once came to within ten yards of me and did not strike. I am a strange man and do not know what's wrong with me. But I know how to fix myself when I am broken. You must change your life, Rilke said, and now I am changing mine. Who knows, when I come to my senses, somebody will have taken my job and I'll be on the streets writing travel articles. So be it. In the meantime I am destined to study science and I am going to study science. I cannot allow this body of information to pass me by and I can't concentrate on it while attempting to evaluate Hollywood movies."

Nieman moved closer to the window so he could feel the cold permeating the glass. Small soft flakes were still falling, so light and small it seemed impossible they could have turned the hills so white and covered the trees and the piles of firewood and the well. I can trek out if I have to, he decided. I won't worry about this snow. This snow is here to soothe me. To make the world a wonderland for me to study. Life as a cosmic imperative, de Duve says. I will read that book first, then do three pages of math. I have to learn math. My brain is only forty-four years old, for Christ's sake. Mother taught math. The gene's in there somewhere. It's just rusty. Before there was oxygen there was no rust. Iron existed in the prebiotic oceans in a ferrous state. My brain is like that. There are genes in there that have never been exposed to air. Now I will use them.

Nieman was trembling with the cold and the excitement of the ideas in his head. Proteins and nucleic acids, the idea that all life on earth came from a single cell that was created by a cosmic imperative. Given the earth and the materials of which it is created, life was inevitable. Ever-increasing complexity was also inevitable. It was inevitable that we would create nuclear energy, inevitable that we would overpopulate the earth. It was not as insane as it had always seemed. And perhaps it was not as inevitable once the mind could recognize and grasp the process.

Nieman heaved a great happy sigh. He left watching the snow and turned and climbed the ladder to the sleeping loft. There, on that bed, in that corner beneath the skylight, on a freezing night ten years before, Freddy and Nora Jane's twins had been born, his surrogate children, his goddaughters, his angels, his dancing princesses. Nieman lay down upon the bed and thought about the twins and the progress of their lives. Not everything ends in tragedy, he decided. My life has not been tragic, neither has Freddy's or Nora Jane's. Perhaps the world will last another hundred years. Perhaps this safety can be stretched to include the lives of Tammili and Lydia. So what if they are not mine, not related to me. All life comes from one cell. They are mine because they have my heart. It is theirs. I belong to them, have pondered over them and loved them for ten years. How can this new knowledge I want to acquire help them? How can this new birth of curiosity and wonder add to the store of goodness in the world?

Well, Nieman, don't be a fool. It isn't up to you to solve the problems of the world. But it might be. There were ninety-two people in that lecture room but I was the only one who had this violent a reaction to what the professor was saying. I was the only one who took what he was saying as a blow to the solar plexus. This might be my mission. It might be up to me to learn this stuff and pass it on. It is not inevitable that we overpopulate and destroy the world. Knowledge is still power. Knowledge will save us.

Nieman was crying. He lay on the bed watching the snow falling on the skylight and tears rolled down his face and filled his ears and got his fringe of hair soaking wet. He cried and he allowed himself to cry.

I had thought it was art, he decided. Certainly art is part of it. Cro-Magnon man mixing earth with saliva and spitting it on the walls of caves was a biochemist. He was taking the elements he found around him and using them to explore and recreate and enlarge his grasp of reality. After the walls were painted he could come back and stare at them and wonder at what he had created. Perhaps he cried out, terrified by the working of his mind and hands. I might stare in such a manner at this house we built. I could go outside and watch the snow falling on those primitive solar panels we installed so long ago. It is all one, our well and solar panels and the cave paintings at Lascaux and microscopes at Berkeley and this man in Belgium writing this book to blow my mind wide open and Lydia and Tammili carrying their backpacks to school each morning. The maker of this bed and the ax that felled the trees that made the boards we hammered and Jonas Salk and murderers and thieves and Akira Kurosawa and Abraham Pais and I are one. This great final truth, which all visionaries have intuited, which must be learned over and over again, world without end, amen.

Nieman fell asleep. The snow fell faster. The flakes were larger now, coming from a cloud of moisture that had once been the Mediterranean Sea, that had filled the wells of Florence, in the time of Leonardo da Vinci, and his royal patron, Francis, King of France.

The young man was wearing long robes of dark red and brown. His hair was wild and curly and his feet were in leather sandals. His face was tanned and his eyes were as blue as the sky. He had been knocking on the door for many minutes when Nieman came to consciousness and climbed down the ladder to let him in. "Come in," Nieman said. "I was asleep. Are you lost? I'm Nieman Gluuk. Come in and warm yourself."

"It took a while to get here," the young man said. "That's a kind fire you have going."

"Sit down. Do you live around here? Could I get you something to drink? Coffee or tea or brandy? Could I get you a glass of water? We have a well. Perhaps you're hungry." The young man moved into the living room and looked around with great interest. He walked over to the window and laid his palms against the glass. Then he touched it with his cheek. He smiled at that and turned back to Nieman.

"Food would be nice. Bread or cheese. I'll sit by the fire and warm myself."

Nieman went into the kitchen and began to get out food and a water glass. The young man picked up the book by the biochemist de Duve, and began to read it, turning the pages very quickly. His eyes would move across the page, then he would turn the page. By the time Nieman returned to the fireplace with a tray, the young man had turned half the pages. "This is a fine book," he said to Nieman, smiling and taking a piece of bread from the tray. "It would be worth the trip to read this."

"You aren't from around here, are you?" Nieman asked.

"You know who I am. You called me here. Don't be frightened. I come when I am truly called. Of course, I can't stay long. I would like to finish this book now. It won't take long. Do you have something to do while I'm reading?" The young man smiled a dazzling smile at Nieman. It was the face of the Angel of the Annunciation in Leonardo's painting. It was the face of David. "You knew me, didn't you?" the young man added. "Weren't there things you wanted to tell me?"

Nieman walked back toward the kitchen, breathing very softly. The young man's face, his hair, his feet, his hands. It was all as familiar as the face Nieman saw every day in the mirror when he shaved. Nieman let his hands drop to his sides. He stood motionless by the ladder while the young man finished reading the book.

"What should I call you?" Nieman said at last.

"Francis called me da Vinci."

"How do you speak English?"

"That's the least of the problems."

"What is the most?"

"Jarring the protoplasm. Of course, I only travel when it's worth it. I will have a whole day. Is there something you want to show me?"

"I want to take you to the labs at Berkeley. I want to show you the microscopes and telescopes, but I guess that's nothing to what you've seen by now. I could tell you about them. Did you really just read that book?"

"Yes. It's very fine, but why did he waste so many pages pretending to entertain superstitious ideas? Are ideas still subject to the Church in this time?"

"It's more subtle, but they're there. The author probably didn't want to seem superior. That's big now."

"I used to do that. Especially with Francis. He was so needy. We will go to your labs if you like. Or we could walk in this snow. I only came to keep you company. It's your time." He smiled again, a smile so radiant that it transported Nieman outside his fear that he was losing his mind.

"Why to me?"

"Because you might be lonely in the beginning. Afterward, you will have me if you need me." The young man folded the book very carefully and laid it on a cushion. "Tell me how cheese is made now," he said, beginning to eat the food slowly and carefully as he talked. "How is it manufactured? What are the cows named? Who wraps it? How is it transported?"

"The Pacific Ocean is near here," Nieman answered. He had taken a seat a few feet from the young man. "We might be able to get out in the Jeep. That's the vehicle out there. Gasoline powered. I don't know what you know and what you don't know. Do you want to read some more books?"

"Could we go to this ocean?"

"I guess we could. I have hiking gear. If we can't get through we can always make it back. I have a mobile phone. I'd like to watch you read another book. I have a book of algebra and a book that is an overview of where we are in the sciences now. There's a book of plays and plenty of poetry. I'd be glad to sit here and read with you. But finish eating. Let me get you some fruit to go with that."

"Give me the books. I will read them."

Nieman got up and collected books from around the room and brought them and put them beside the young man. Then he brought in firewood and built up the fire. He took a book of poetry and sat near the young man and read as the young man read. Here is the poem he turned to and the one he kept reading over and over again as he sat by the young man's side with the fire roaring and the wind picking up outside and the snow falling faster and faster.

> . . . Still, if love torments you so much and you so much need
> To sail the Stygian lake twice and twice to inspect
> The murk of Tartarus, if you will go beyond the limit,
> Understand what you must do beforehand.
> Hidden in the thick of a tree is a bough made of gold
> And its leaves and pliable twigs are made of it too.
> It is sacred to underworld Juno, who is its patron,
> And it is roofed in by a grove, where deep shadows mass
> Along far wooded valleys. No one is ever permitted

To go down to earth's hidden places unless he has first
Plucked this golden-fledged growth out of its tree
And handed it over to fair Proserpina, to whom it belongs
By decree, her own special gift. And when it is plucked,
A second one always grows in its place, golden again,
And the foliage growing on it has the same metal sheen.
Therefore look up and search deep and when you have found it,
Take hold of it boldly and duly. If fate has called you,
The bough will come away easily, of its own accord.
Otherwise, no matter how much strength you muster,
You never will
Manage to quell it or cut it down with
The toughest of blades.

"Now," the young man said, when he finished the biochemistry textbook. "Tell me about these infinitesimal creatures, amoebas, proteins, acid chains, slime molds, white cells, nuclei, enzymes, DNA, RNA, atoms, quarks, strings, and so on. What an army they have found. I could not have imagined it was that complicated. They have seen these creatures? Many men have seen them?"

"We have telescopes and microscopes with lenses ground a million times to such fineness and keenness, with light harnessed from electrons. They can magnify a million times. A thousand million. I don't know the numbers. I can take you to where they are. I can take you to see them if you want to go."

"Of course. Yes, you will take me there. But it must be soon. There is a limited amount of time I will be with you."

"How much time?"

"It will suffice. Will your vehicle travel in this snow?"

"Yes. Perhaps you would like to borrow some modern clothes. Not that there's anything wrong with your clothes. They are very nice. I was especially admiring the cape. The weave is lovely. They're always worrying about security. I want to take you to the laboratories at Berkeley. I can call the head of the department. He will let us in."

"You may have the cloak since you admire it. It can remain

here." He removed the long brown garment and handed it to Nieman.

"I'll give you a parka." Nieman ran for the coat rack and took down a long beige parka Freddy had ordered from L.L. Bean. He held it out to the young man. "I guess I seem nervous. I'm not. It's just that I've wanted to talk to you since I was ten years old."

"Yes. You've been calling me for some time."

"I thought you would be old. Like of the time when you died. Did you die?"

"I thought so. It was most uncomfortable and Francis wept like a child, which was not altogether unpleasant." He laughed softly. "It is better to come with my young eyes. In case there is something to see."

"Where are you when you aren't here?"

"Quite far away."

"Will it matter that you came here? I mean in the scheme of things, as it were?"

"It will matter to me. To read the books and see these instruments you are describing. I have always wished to have my curiosity satisfied. That was always what I most dreamed of doing. Francis never understood that. He could never believe I wouldn't be satisfied to eat and drink and be lauded and talk with him. It kept me from loving him as he deserved."

"I meant, will it change the course of anything?"

"Not unless you do it."

"I wouldn't do it. Could I do it by accident?"

"No. I will see to that. Do you want to go out now, in the vehicle in the snow?" There it was again, the smile that soaked up all the light and gave it back.

"Let's get dressed for it." Nieman led his guest upstairs and gave him a warm shirt and socks and shoes and pants and long underwear. While he was changing Nieman banked the fire and put the food away and set the crumbs out for the birds and locked the windows and threw his things into a bag. He forgot to drain the pipes.

"Well, now," he said out loud. "I guess I can drive that Jeep

in this snow. Let's assume I can drive. Let's say it's possible and
I will do it." He turned on the mobile phone and called the
department at Berkeley and left a message saying he was bringing a senator to see the labs. Then he called the president of the
university at his home and called in his markers. "Very hush-
hush," he told the president. "This could be very big, Joe. This
could be millions for research but you have to trust me. Don't
ask questions. Just tell the grounds people to give me the keys
when I come ask for them. I can't tell you who it is. You have to
trust me."

"Of course, Nieman," the president answered. "After everything you and Freddy have done for us. Anything you want."

"The keys to everything. The electron microscopes, the physics labs, the works. We could use one of your technical people
for a guide but no one else."

"There'll be people working in the labs."

"I know that. We won't bother anyone. I'll call you Monday
and tell you more."

"Fine. I'll look forward to hearing about it." After he hung
up the phone the university president said to his wife. "That
was Nieman Gluuk. Did you know he's quitting writing his
column? Took a leave of absence to go back to school."

"Well, don't you go getting any ideas like that," his good-looking wife giggled. "All he ever wrote about were foreign films.
He'd gotten brutal in his reviews. Maybe they let him go. Maybe
he just pretended that he quit."

There was a layer of ice beneath the snow. Nieman tested it by
walking on it, then put Leonardo into the passenger seat and
buckled him in and got behind the wheel and started driving.
He drove very carefully in the lowest gear across the rock-strewn
yard toward the wooden gate that fenced in nothing since the
fence had been abandoned as a bad idea. "Thank God it's
downhill," he said. "It's downhill most of the way to the main
road. So, when was the last time you were here?" He talked
without turning his head. The sun was out now. Birds were
beginning to circle above the huge fir trees in the distance.
"Have you been to the United States? To the West Coast?"

"Once long ago. I saw the ocean with a man of another race. I walked beside it and felt its power. It is different from the ocean I knew."

"We can go there first. It won't take long once we get to the main road. I'm sorry if I keep asking you questions. I can't help being curious."

"You can ask them if you like. I was visited by Aristotle in my turn. We went to a river and explored its banks. He was very interested in my studies of moving water. He said the flow of water would impede the mixture of liquids and we talked of how liquid forms its boundaries within a flow. He had very beautiful hands. I painted them later from memory several times. Of course everyone thought they were Raphael's hands. Perhaps I thought so too finally. After he left I had no real memory of it for a while. More like the memory of a dream, bounded, uncertain, without weight. I think it will be like that for you, so ask whatever you wish to ask."

"I don't think I want to ask anything now. I think we should go to the ocean first since we are so near. I forget about water. I forget to look at it with clear eyes, and yet I was watching the snow when I fell asleep. Also, I was crying. Why are you smiling?"

"Go on."

"I was thinking that when I was small I knew how to appreciate the ocean. Later, I forgot. When I was small I would stand in one place for a very long time watching the waves lap. Every day I came back to the same spot. I made footprints for the waves to wash away. I made castles farther and farther up the beach to see how far the tide could reach. I dug into the sand, as deep as it would allow me to dig. I was an infatuate of ocean, wave, beach. Are you warm enough? Is that coat comfortable?"

"I am warm. Tell me about this vehicle. What do you call it?"

"Automobile. Like auto and mobile. It's a Jeep, a four-wheel drive. We call it our car. Everyone has one. We work for them. We fight wars over the fuel to power them. We spend a lot of time in them. They have radios. We listen to broadcasts from around the world while we drive. Or we listen to taped books. I have a book of the Italian language we could listen to. You might want to see how it's evolved. It might be the same. It might be quite similar to what you spoke. Would you like to hear it?" Nieman shifted into a higher gear. The road was still steep but lay in the lee of the mountain and was not iced beneath the snow. "We'll be on the main road, soon," he added. "We're in luck it seems. I wouldn't have driven this alone. One more question. How do you read the books so fast?"

"I'm not sure." Leonardo laughed. "It's been going on since I quit the other life. It's getting better. At first it was not this fast. I'm very fond of being able to do it. It's the nicest thing of all."

"Where do you stay? When you aren't visiting? I mean, going someplace like this."

"With other minds."

"Disembodied?"

"If we want to be. Is that the main road?" It was before them, the road to Willits. Plows had pushed the snow in dirty piles on either side of the road. In the center two vehicles were moving in one lane down the mountain. A blue sedan and a white minivan were bouncing down the road in the ripening sunlight.

"I believe this," Nieman said. "I'm in my red Jeep driving Leonardo da Vinci down from the house to see the ocean. My name is Nieman Gluuk and I have striven all my life to be a good man and use my talents and conquer resentment and be glad for whatever fate dumped me in Northern California the only child of a bitter woman and a father I almost never saw, and I never went into a movie theater expecting to hate the movie and was saddened when I did. Maybe this is payback and maybe this is chance and maybe I deserve this and the only thing I wish is that my friend, Freddy, could be here so it won't destroy our friendship when I am driven to tell him about it."

"You won't remember it." Leonardo reached over and touched his sleeve. He smiled the dazzling smile again and Nieman took it in without driving off the road and took the last curve down onto the highway. "You will have it," Leonardo added. "It is yours, but you won't have the burden of remembering it."

"I want the burden." Nieman laughed. "Burden me. Try me. I

can take it. I'll write a movie script and publicize intelligence. *Nel mezzo del cammin di nostra vita mi ritrovai per una selva oscura, che la diritta via era smarrita. Ahi quanto a dir qual era e cosa dura esta selva selvaggia e aspra e forte.* That's the beginning of *The Divine Comedy.* That's what I went back to Berkeley to take. Instead, I'm in this forest of biochemistry. I'm dreaming the things I'm reading. They put literature into a new light. The artist intuits what the mind knows and the mind knows everything, doesn't it? Past, present, and forevermore."

"Some wake to it gradually. Some never know."

"I've worked for it," Nieman said. "I have worked all my life to understand, to see myself as the product of five hundred million years of evolution. You seem to have known it always."

"I was taken from my mother's house when I was four years old. On the walk to my father's house, the fields and the wonder of the earth came to console me. But I worked also. I always worked." He laid his hand on Nieman's arm. Nieman steered the Jeep across a pile of snow and turned onto the road leading down to Willits. Around them the snow-covered hills with their massive fir trees were paintings of unspeakable complexity. Neither of them spoke for many miles.

It was past noon when they drove through the small town of Willits and turned onto Highway 20 leading to the Pacific Ocean. "I'm going to stop for gasoline for the automobile," Nieman said. "We collect it in foreign countries. The countries of the Turks and Muslims, although some of it is under the ground of this country. We store it underneath these filling stations in large steel tanks. Steel is an alloy made of iron and carbon. It's very strong. Then we drive up to the pumping stations and pump the fuel into our tanks. Even young children do this, Leonardo. I don't know what you know and what you don't know, but I feel I should explain some things."

"I like to hear you speak of these phenomena. Continue. I will listen and watch."

Nieman spotted a Conoco station and stopped the Jeep and got out. He took down one of the gasoline hoses and inserted it in the fuel tank of the Jeep. Leonardo stood beside the tank watching and not speaking. "Don't smile that smile at anyone else," Nieman said. "We'll be arrested for doing hallucinogens."

"They never explode?" Leonardo moved in for a closer look, took a sniff of the fumes, then put both hands in the pockets of the jacket. There was a package of Kleenex in one pocket. He brought it out and examined it.

"It's called Kleenex. We blow our noses on it," Nieman explained. "It's a disposable handkerchief."

"Could one draw on it?" Leonardo held a sheet up to the light. "It's fragile and thin."

"Wait a minute." Nieman pulled a notepad and a black felt-tip pen out of the glove compartment and handed them to Leonardo. Leonardo examined the pen, took the top from it, and began to draw, leaning the pad against the top of the Jeep. Nieman put the hose back on the pump, then went inside and paid for the gasoline. When he returned, Leonardo had covered a page with the smallest, most precise lines Nieman had ever seen. Leonardo handed the drawing to him. It was of the mountains and the trees. In the foreground Nieman was standing beside the Jeep with the gasoline hose in his hand.

Nieman took the drawing and held it. "You are a microscope," he said. "Perhaps you will not be impressed with the ones we've made."

"Shall we continue on our way?" Leonardo asked. "Now that your tank is full of gasoline."

They drove in silence for a while. The sun was out in full violence now, melting the snow and warming the air. "The air is an ocean of currents," Nieman said at last. "I suppose you know about that."

"Always good to be reminded of anything we know."

"You want to hear the Italian tape? I'd like to hear what you think of it."

"That would be fine."

Nieman reached into a pack of tapes and extracted the Beginning Italian tape and stuck it into the tape player. "This Jeep doesn't have very good speakers," he said. "We have systems that are much better than this one." The Italian teacher began to teach Italian phrases. Leonardo began to laugh. Quietly at first, then louder and louder until he was shaking with laughter.

"What's so funny?" Nieman asked. He was laughing too. "What do you think is funny? Why am I laughing too?"

"Such good jokes," Leonardo answered, continuing to laugh. "What questions. What news. What jokes."

It was thirty-six miles from Willits to the Pacific Ocean. The road led down between mountains and virgin forests. They drove along at fifty miles an hour, listening to the Italian tape and then to Kiri Te Kanawa singing arias from Italian opera. Nieman was lecturing Leonardo on the history of opera and its great modern stars. Long afterward, when he had forgotten everything about the day that could be proven, Nieman remembered the drive from Willits to the ocean and someone beside him laughing. "Are you sure you weren't with me?" he asked Freddy a hundred times later in their lives. "Maybe we were stoned. But Kiri Te Kanawa didn't start recording until after we had straightened up so we couldn't have been stoned. I think you were with me. You just don't remember it."

"I never drove in a Jeep with you from Willits to the ocean while listening to Italian tapes. I would remember that, Nieman. Why do you always ask me that? It's a loose wire in your head, a precursor of dreaded things to come." Then Freddy would smile and shake his head and later talk about it to his psychiatrist or Nora Jane. "Nieman's fixated on thinking I drove with him in a Jeep listening to an Italian tape," he would say. "About once a year he starts on that. It's like the budding of the trees. Once a year, in winter, he decides the two of us took that trip and nothing will convince him otherwise. He gets mad at me because I can't remember it. Can you believe it?"

Outside the small town of Novo, Nieman found a trail he had used before. It led to a beach the townspeople used during good weather. He parked the Jeep in a gravel clearing and they got out and climbed down a path to the water. The ocean was very dramatic, with huge boulders jutting into the entrance of a small harbor. The snow was melting on the path. Even now, in the heart of winter, moss was forming on the rocks. "'The force that through the green fuse drives the flower,'" Nieman said.

"Dylan is happy now," Leonardo answered. "A charming man. I go to him quite often and he recites poetry. It makes the poetry he wrote when he was here seem primitive. I should not tell you that, of course. We try never to say such things."

"Look at the ocean," Nieman answered. "What mystery could be greater. Shouldn't this be enough for any man to attempt to understand? This force, this power, this place where land and air meet the sea? '. . . this goodly frame, the earth . . . this most excellent canopy, the air . . . this brave o'erhanging firmament, this majestical roof fretted with golden fire . . .'"

"Will loved the sea and wrote of it but had little time for it. Plato was the same. He talked and wrote of it but didn't take the time to ponder it as we are doing. Of course, in other ages time seemed more valuable. Life was short and seemed more fleeting."

They were walking along a strip of sand only ten to twenty feet wide. It was low tide. Later in the day it would have been impossible to walk here and they would have had to use the higher path.

"We could just stay here," Nieman said. "We don't have to go to the labs. I just thought you might want to see the microscopes."

"We have all day."

"They're leaving the labs open in the biochemistry building. We can go to Berkeley or we can stay here. I saw you looking at the atlas. Did you memorize it? I mean, is that how you do it?"

"I remember it. It is very fine how they have mapped the floor of the oceans. Is it exact, do you think?"

"Pretty much so at the time of mapping. The sand shifts, everything shifts and changes. They map the floor with soundings, with radar. When you leave here, where do you have to be? Is there some gathering place? Do you just walk off? Where do you go?"

"I just won't be here."

"Will the clothes be here? I only wondered. That's Freddy's coat. I could get him another one but he's pretty fond of that one. He took it to Tibet."

Nieman moved nearer to Leonardo, his eyes shifting wildly. The day had a sort of rhythm. Sometimes it was just beating along. Then suddenly he imagined it whole and that made his heart beat frantically. "I don't care, of course. You can take it if you need to. You can have anything I have."

"I will leave the clothes. It would be a waste to take them."

"When will you go? How long will it be? You have to understand. I never had a father. No man ever stayed long enough. I was always getting left on my own. It's been a problem for me all my life."

Leonardo turned to face him. "This is not a father who leaves, Nieman. This is the realm of knowledge, which you always longed for and long for now. It is always available, it never goes away, it cannot desert you, it cannot fail you. It is yours. It belongs to whoever longs for it. If you desert it, it is always waiting, like those waves. It comes back and back like the sea. I am only a moment of what is available to you. When I am gone the clothes will be here and you can wear them when you are reading things that are difficult to understand. You will read everything now. You will learn many languages. You will know much more than you know now. Tell me about the microscopes."

"I haven't used one yet. But I can tell you how it works. It concentrates a beam of electrons in a tube to scan or penetrate the thing you want magnified. It makes a photograph using light and dark and shadow. The photograph is very accurate and magnified a million times. Then a portion of that photograph can be magnified several million more times. It's so easy for me to believe the photographs so I think it must be something I know. My friend, Freddy, thinks we know everything back to the first cell, that all discovery is simply plugging into memory banks. Memory at the level of biochemistry. Which is why I can't believe it took me so long to begin to study this. I had to start in the arts. My mother is a frustrated actress. I've been working her program for forty-four years. Now it's my turn. But this is plain to you. You're the one who saw the relationship between art and science. It never occurred to you not to do both."

"I am honored to be here for your birth of understanding. Where I am, the minds are past their early enthusiasms. I miss seeing the glint in eyes. I miss the paintbrush in my hand and the smell of paints. If you wish to show me this microscope we can go there now. The sea is very old. We don't have to stay beside it all day."

It was a two-and-a-half-hour drive to Berkeley. They drove along the western ridge of the Cascade Range, within a sea breeze of the Mendocino Fracture Zone. Beside the Russian River. They drove to Mendocino, then Littleriver, then Albion. At Albion they cut off onto Highway 128 and drove along the Navarro River to Cloverdale. They went by Santa Rosa, then Petaluma, then Novato, and down and across the Richmond–San Rafael Bridge and on to Berkeley.

It was six o'clock when they arrived at the campus. It was dark and the last students were mounting their bicycles as they left the biochemistry building. Nieman nosed the Jeep into a faculty parking space and they got out and entered the building through iron doors and went down a hall to an elevator.

"Have you been on one of these?" Nieman asked, holding the elevator door with his hand. "It's a box on a pulley, actually. It's quite safe. When they were new sometimes they would get stuck. Some pretty funny jokes and stories came out of that. Also, there were tragedies, lack of oxygen and so forth. This one is thirty years old at least, but it's safe."

"Arabic," Leonardo said, touching the numbered buttons with his finger. "I thought it would continue to be useful."

"The numbers? Oh, yes. Everyone uses the same system. Based on the fingers and toes. Five fingers on each hand. Two arms, two legs. Binary system and digital system. We run our computers on the binary system. It's fascinating. What man has done. There's one playwright dealing with it, a man named Stoppard." Leonardo stepped back and stood near Nieman. Nieman pressed 2 and the box rose in space on its pulley and the door opened.

Waiting for them on the second-floor hall was the head of university security. He was wearing a blue uniform with silver buttons. "Hello," he said. "If you're Mr. Gluuk they have a lady waiting for you. President Culver said to tell you she'd show you the machines."

"Oh, that wasn't necessary. We only wanted to look at them." He took Leonardo's arm. So he looks like a genius who has spent a thousand years on a Buddhist prayer bench. So the smile is so dazzling it hypnotizes people. No one would imagine this. No one would believe it.

"Don't I know you from when I was a student?" Nieman asked. "I'm Nieman Gluuk. I used to edit the school paper. In the seventies. Didn't you guard the building when we had the riots in seventy-five?"

"I thought I knew you. I'm Abel Kennedy. I was a rookie that year and you kept me supplied with cookies and coffee in the newspaper office. I'm head of security now." Captain Kennedy held out his hand and Nieman shook it. He was trying to decide how to introduce Leonardo when a door opened down the hall and a woman came walking toward them. She was of medium height with short blond hair. She was wearing a pair of blue jeans and a long-sleeved white shirt. Over the shirt was a long white vest. There were pencils and pens in the pockets of the vest. A pair of horn-rimmed glasses was on her head. Another pair was in her hand.

"I was wondering if one could wear bifocals to look into the scope," Nieman said. "I was afraid I'd have to get contact lenses to study science."

"It's a screen." She laughed. "I'm Stella Light. My parents were with the Merry Pranksters. Some joke. I meant to have it changed but I never did." She held out her hand to Nieman. Long slender fingers. Nails bitten off to the quick. No rings. She smiled again.

"I'm Nieman Gluuk. This is our distinguished guest, Leo Gluuk, a cousin from Madrid. I mean, Florence. Also from Minneapolis."

"Make up your mind. Nice to meet you. I've read your stuff. I'm from Western Oregon. Well, what exactly can we do for you?"

"Just let us see the microscopes. Leo is very interested in the technology. It's extremely nice of you to stay late like this. I know your days are long enough already."

"I was here anyway. We've had an outbreak of salmonella in the valley. We're trying to help out with that. It gets on the chicken skin in the packing plants or if they are defrosted incorrectly. Well, I'll let you see slides of that. They're fresh."

They walked down a hall to a room with the door ajar. Inside, on a long curved table, was the console. In the center, covered with a metal that looked more like gold than brass, was the scanning electron microscope. The pride of the Berkeley labs.

They moved into the open doorway. Leonardo had been completely quiet. Now he gave Stella the smile and she stepped back and let him precede her into the room. She and Leonardo sat down at the console. She got out a box of slides and lifted one from the box with a set of calipers. She slid it into a notch and locked it down. Then she pushed a button and an image appeared on the screen. "To 0.2 nanometers," she said. "We can photograph it and go higher."

Nieman leaned over their shoulders and looked into the screen. It was a range of hills covered with cocoons. "A World War I battlefield," he said. "Corpses strewn everywhere. Is that the salmonella?"

"Yes. Let's enlarge it." She pushed another button. The hill turned into crystal mountains. Now it was the Himalayas. Range after range of crystals. Nieman looked down at his own arm. In a nanometer of skin was all that wonder.

Leonardo began asking questions about the machine, about the metal of which it was made, about the vacuum through which the electrons traveled, how the image was created. Stella answered the questions as well as she could. She bent over him. She put pieces of paper in front of him. She put slides into the microscope. She asked no questions. She had been completely mesmerized by the smile. She would remember nothing of the encounter. Except a momentary excitement when she was alone in the room at night. She thought it was sexual. She thought it was about Nieman. There I go, she would scold herself, getting interested in yet another man I cannot understand. The daddy track, chugging on down the line to lonesome valley.

They stayed in the laboratory for half an hour. Then they wandered out into the hall and found a second microscope and Stella took the thing apart and let Leonardo examine the parts. Then she let him reassemble it. She stood beside Nieman. She sized him up. He was better looking than his photograph in the paper. His skin was so white and clear. He was kind.

"You really quit your job?" she asked.

"A leave of absence. I was burned out."

"Who is he?" she asked. "I don't think I've ever met anyone I liked as much."

"We all love him. The family adores him. But it's hard to keep track of him. He travels all the time."

Leonardo put everything back into its place. He laid Stella's pencil on top of the stack of papers and got up from the chair. "We are finished now," he said. "We should be leaving. We thank you for your kindness."

Stella walked them to the elevator. They got on and she stood smiling after them. When they had left she went back into the laboratory and worked until after twelve. Two children had died in the salmonella outbreak. Twenty were hospitalized. The infected food had reached a grade school lunchroom.

When they left the building there was a full moon in the sky. There was so much light it cast shadows. Leonardo walked with Nieman to the Jeep. "I am leaving," he said. "You will be fine." He kissed Nieman on the cheek, then on the forehead. Then he was gone. Nieman tried to follow him but he did not know how. When he got back to the Jeep, the clothes Leonardo had been wearing were neatly stacked on the passenger seat. On top of the clothes was a pencil. A black and white striped pencil sharpened to a fine point. Nieman picked it up and held it. He put it in his pocket. I might write with this, he decided. Or I might draw.

He got into his Jeep and drove over to Nora Jane and Freddy Harwood's house and parked in the driveway and walked up on the porch and rang the doorbell. The twins let him in. They pulled him into the room. "Momma's making étouffée and listening to the Nevilles," Tammili told him. "She's having a New Orleans day. Come on in. Stay and eat dinner with us. Daddy said you'd been in Willits. How is it there? Was it snowing?"

They dragged him into the house. From the back Freddy called out to him. Nora Jane emerged from the kitchen wearing an apron. It was already beginning to fade. Whatever had happened or almost happened or seemed to happen was fading like a photograph in acid.

"Come on in here," Freddy was calling out. "Come tell us what you were doing. We have things to tell you. Tammili made all-stars in basketball. Lydia got a role in the school play. Nora Jane got an A on her first English test. I think I'm going bald. We haven't seen you in days. Hurry up, Nieman. I want to talk to you."

"He's your best friend," Lydia giggled, half whispering. "It's so great. You just love each other."

The Brown Cape

TAMMILI AND LYDIA were supposed to be cleaning up the loft.
Their father was working on the well. Their mother was cooking
breakfast and it was their job to make the beds and straighten
up the loft and clean the windows with vinegar and water.

"Why can't we clean them with Windex like we do at home?"
Lydia complained. "Just because we come to Willits for spring
vacation they go environmental and we have to use vinegar for
the windows. The windows are okay. I'm not cleaning them."

"You shouldn't have come then. You could have stayed with
Grandmother. You didn't have to come if you're just going to
complain."

"Why can't we have a ski lodge or something? Why do we
have to have a solar house? We can't bring anybody. It's too little
to even bring the dogs."

"It's a solar-powered house, not a solar house, and I don't
want to take dogs everywhere I go. There're wolves and panthers
in these woods. Those dogs wouldn't last a week up here. Dooley
is so friendly he'd let a wolf carry him off in his teeth."

"You clean the windows and I'll get all this stuff out from
under the bed. Everyone's always sticking stuff under here. I
hate piles of junk like this." Lydia was pulling boxes and clothes

out from underneath the bed where she and Tammili had been sleeping. It was the bed on which they had been born, in the middle of the night, ten and a half years before. Their father had delivered them and a helicopter had come and taken them to a hospital at Fort Bragg. Sometimes Lydia felt sentimental about that and sometimes she didn't like to think about it. It was embarrassing to have been delivered in a snowstorm by your father. Not to mention they had almost died. That was too terrible to think about.

"What are you thinking about?" Tammili asked, but she knew. She and Lydia always thought about things at the same time. It was the curse and blessing of being twins. You were never lonely, not even in your thoughts. On the other hand there was no place to hide.

"Who put this here?" Lydia dragged a long brown cloak out from underneath the bed. It had a cowl and a twisted cord for the waist and it was very thick, as thick as a blanket. It smelled heavenly, like some wonderful mixture of wildflowers and mist. She pulled it out and spread it on the bed. Then she wrapped it around her shoulders.

"I've never seen this before." Tammili drew near the cape and touched it. "It smells like violet. I bet it belongs to Nieman. No one but Nieman would leave a cape here. Let me wear it too, will you?" She moved into one half of the cape. They wrapped it around themselves like a cocoon and fell down on the bed and started laughing.

"Once upon a time," Lydia began, "there were two little girls and they were so poor they didn't have any firewood for the fireplace. All the trees had been cut down by ruthless land developers and there weren't any twigs left to gather to make a fire. They only had one thing left and that was their bed. We better cut up the bed and burn it, one of them said, or else we won't live until the morning. We will freeze to death in this weather. Okay, the other one said. Pull that bed over here and let's burn it up. Then they saw something under the bed. It was a long warm cape that their father had left for them when he went away to war. There was a note on it. 'This is for my darling daughters in case they run out of firewood. Love, your dad.'"

"Tammili." It was their mother calling. "You girls come on down. I want you to help me with the eggs." Tammili and Lydia put their faces very close together. They giggled again, smothering the sound.

"We're coming," Lydia called. "We'll be down in a minute." They folded the cape and laid it on the bed by Tammili's backpack. Then they climbed down the ladder to help their mother with the meal.

That was Wednesday morning. On Wednesday night their father decided they should go on an expedition. "To where?" their mother asked. "You know I have to study while I'm here. I can't go off for days down a river or in the mountains. One-day trips. That's all I'm good for this week."

"I thought we might overnight up in the pass by Red River," Freddy Harwood said. "Nieman and I used to camp there every spring. It might be cold but we'll take the bedrolls and I'll have the mobile phone. You can't go for one night?"

"I should stay here. Do you need me?"

"We don't need you," Tammili said. "We can take care of things. I want to go, Dad. We've been hearing about Red River for years but no one ever takes us. We're almost eleven. We can do anything."

"Get another adult," Nora Jane insisted. "Don't go off with both of them and no one to help."

"We are help," Lydia said. "Is it a steep climb, Daddy? Is it steep?"

"No. It's long but it's not that steep. Nieman and I used to do the trail to the top in three hours. Two and a half coming down. There's a bower up there under thousand-year-old pine trees. You don't need a sleeping bag. We'll take them but we could sleep on the ground. I haven't been up there to camp in years. Not since I met your mother. So, we'll go. It's decided."

"Tomorrow," they both screamed.

"Maybe tomorrow. Maybe Friday. Let me think about it." They jumped on top of him and started giving him one of their famous hug attacks. They grabbed pillows and hugged him with them until he screamed for mercy. "Tomorrow, tomorrow, tomorrow," they kept saying. "Don't make us wait."

"Then we have to get everything ready tonight because we have to leave at sunup. It takes an hour to drive to the trail. Then three hours to climb. I want to have camp set up by afternoon."

"What do we need?"

"Tent, food, clothes, extra socks. Vaseline for blisters, ankle packs for sprains, snakebite kit, Mag Lites, sleeping bags."

"We're going to carry all that?"

"Whatever we want we have to carry. We'll have extra water in the car. We'll take small canteens and the purifying kit. Go start pumping at the well, Tammili. Fill two water bags."

"Can't I fill them at the sink?"

"No, the idea is to know how to survive without a sink. That's what Willits is for, sweeties."

"We know." They gave each other a look. "So no matter what happens your DNA is safe." They started giggling and their mother put down the dish she was drying and started giggling too.

Freddy Harwood was an equipment freak. He had spent the summers of his youth in wilderness camps in Montana and western Canada. When he graduated to camping on his own, he took up equipment as a cause. If he was going camping he had every state-of-the-art device that could be ordered on winter nights from catalogs. He had Mag Lites on headbands and Bull Frog sunblock. He had wrist compasses and Ray-Ban sunglasses and Power Bars and dehydrated food. He had two lightweight tents, a Stretch Dome and a Lookout. The Lookout was the lightest. It weighed five pounds, fifteen ounces with the poles. He had Patagonia synchilla blankets and official referee whistles and a Pur water purifier and drinking water tablets in case the purifier broke. He had two-bladed knives for the girls and a six-bladed knife for himself. He had stainless-steel pans and waterproofing spray and tent repair kits and first aid kits of every kind.

"Bring everything we think we need and put it on the table," Freddy said. "Then we'll decide what to take and what to leave. Bring everything. Your boots and the clothes you're going to wear. It's eight o'clock. We have to be packed and in bed by ten if we're going in the morning."

The girls went upstairs and picked out clothes to wear. "I'm taking this cape," Tammili said. "I've got a feeling about this cape. I think it's supposed to go to Red River with us."

"Nieman saw baby panthers up there once," Lydia added. "The mother didn't kill him for looking at them she was so weak with hunger because there had been a drought and a forest fire. Nieman left them all his food. He got to within twenty feet of their burrow and put the food where she could get it. Dad was there. He knows it's true. Nieman's so cool. I wish he was going with us."

"He has to study. He's going for a Nobel prize in biochemistry. That's what Dad told Grandmother. He said Nieman wouldn't rest until he won a Nobel."

The girls brought their clothes and backpacks down from the loft and spread the things out on the table. "What's this?" Freddy asked, picking up the cloak.

"Something we found underneath the bed. We think it's Nieman's. I was going to take it instead of a sleeping bag. Look how warm it is."

"I wouldn't carry it if I were you. You have to think of every ounce." Tammili went over and took the cape from him and folded it and laid it on the hearth. Later, when they had finished packing all three of the backpacks and set them by the kitchen door, she picked up the cape and pushed it into her pack. I'm taking it, she decided. I like it. It looks like the luckiest thing you could wear.

In a small, neat condominium in Berkeley, the girls' godfather, Nieman Gluuk, was finishing the last of twenty algebra problems he had set himself for the day. His phone was off the hook. His flower gardens were going wild. His cupboards were bare. His sink was full of dishes. His bed was unmade.

He put the last notation onto the last problem and stood up and began to rub his neck with his hand. He was lonely. His house felt like a tomb. "I'm going to Willits to see the kids," he said out loud. "I'm going crazy all alone in this house. Starting to talk to myself. They are my family and I need them and it's spring vacation and they won't be ten forever."

He went into his bedroom and began to throw clothes into a suitcase. It was three o'clock in the morning. He had been working on the algebra problems for fourteen hours. When Nieman Gluuk set out to conquer a body of knowledge, he did it right. When he had studied philosophy he had learned German and French and Greek. Now he was studying biochemistry and he was learning math. "If my eyes hold out I will learn this stuff," he muttered. "If my eyes give out, I'll learn it with my ears." He pushed the half-filled suitcase onto the floor and turned off the lights and pulled off his shirt and pants and fell into his bed in his underpants. It would be ten in the morning before he woke. Since he had quit his job at the newspaper he had been sleeping nine and ten hours a night. The day he canceled his subscription he slept twelve hours that night.

"The destination," Freddy was saying to his daughters, "is the high caves above Red River. They aren't on this map but you can see the cliff face in these old photographs. Nieman and I took these when we were about twenty years old. We developed them in my old darkroom in Grandmother Ann's house. See all the smudges? We were experimenting with developers." He held the photograph up. "Anyway, we follow the riverbed for a few miles, then up and around the mountain to this pass. Four rivers rise on this mountain. All running west except this one. Red River runs east and north. It's an anomaly, probably left behind from some cataclysm when the earth cooled or else created by an earthquake eons ago. It's unique in every way. If there was enough snow last winter the falls will be spectacular this time of year. Some years they are spectacular and sometimes just a trickle. We won't know until we get there. Even in dry years the sound is great. Where we are camping we will be surrounded by water and the sound of water. It's the best sleeping spot in the world. I'll put it up against any place you can name. I wish your mother was going with us. She doesn't know what she's missing." He took the plate of pancakes Nora Jane handed him and began to eat, lifting each mouthful delicately and dramatically, meeting her violet-blue eyes and saying secrets to her about the night that had passed and the one she was going to be missing.

Tammili and Lydia played with their food. Neither of them could eat when they were excited and they were excited now.

"Is this enough?" Lydia asked her mother. "I really don't want any more."

"Whatever you like. It's a long way to go and the easy way to carry food is in your stomach."

"It weighs the same inside or out," Tammili said. "We're only taking dehydrated packs. In your stomach it's mixed with water so it really weighs less if you carry it in the pack."

Lydia giggled and got up and put her plate by the sink. Tammili followed her. "Let's go," they both said. "Come on, let's get going."

"I wish you had a weather report," Nora Jane put in. "If it turns colder you just come on back."

"Look at that sky. It's as clear as summer. There's nothing moving in today. I've been coming up here for twenty years. I can read this weather like the back of my hand. It's perfect for camping out."

"I know. The world is magic and there's nothing to fear but fear itself." Nora Jane went to her husband and held him in her arms. "Go on and sleep by a waterfall. I wish I could go but I have to finish this paper. That's it. I want to turn it in next week."

"Let's go," Tammili called out. "What's keeping you, Dad? Let's get going." Freddy kissed his wife and went out and got into the driver's seat of the Jeep Cherokee and the girls strapped themselves into the seats behind him and plugged their Walkmans into their ears.

Nora Jane went back into the house and stacked the rest of the dishes by the sink and sat down at the table and got her papers out. She was writing a paper on Dylan Thomas. "'The force that through the green fuse drives the flower / Drives my green age;'" she read, "'that blasts the roots of trees / Is my destroyer. . . .'"

*   *   *

Freddy took a right at the main road to Willits, then turned onto an old gold-mining trail that had been worn down by a hundred years of rain. "Hold on," he told the girls. "This is only for four miles, then we'll be on a better road. It will save us hours if we use this shortcut." The girls took the plugs out of their ears and held on to the seats in front of them. The mobile phone fell from its holder and rattled around on the floor. Tammili captured it and turned it on to see if it was working. "It's broken," she said. "You broke the phone, Dad. It wasn't put back in right."

"Good," he said. "One less hook to civilization. When we get rid of the Jeep we'll be really free. The wilderness doesn't want you to bring a bunch of junk along. It wants you to trust it to provide for you."

"Trusting the earth is trusting yourself. Trusting yourself is trusting the earth. This is our home. We were made for it and it for us." The girls chanted Freddy's credo in unison, then fell into a giggling fit. The Jeep bounced along over the ruts. The girls giggled until they were coughing.

"You have reached the apex of the silly phase," Freddy said, in between the bumps. "You have perfected being ten years old. I don't want this growing up to go a day further. If you get a day older, I'll be mad at you." He gripped the steering wheel, went around a boulder, and came down a steep incline onto a black-top road that curved around and up the mountain. "Okay," he said. "Now we're railroading. Now we're whistling Dixie."

"He hated that mobile phone," Tammili said to her sister. "He's been dying for it to break."

"It's Momma's phone so she can call us from her school," Lydia answered. "He's going to have to get her another one as soon as he gets back."

Nieman woke with a start. He had been dreaming about the equations from the day before. They lined up in front of the newspaper office. Gray uniformed and armed to the teeth, they barred his way to his typewriter. When he tried to reason with them, they held up their guns. They fixed their bayonets.

"I hate dreams," he said. He put his feet down on the floor and looked around at the mess his house was in. He lay back down on the bed. He dialed a number and spoke to the office manager at Merry Maids. Yes, they would send someone to clean the place while he was gone. Yes, they would tell Mr. Levin hello. Yes, they would be sure to come.

I'm out of here, Nieman decided. I'll eat breakfast on the way. They know I'm coming. They know I wouldn't stay away all week. I'll go by the deli and get bagels and smoked salmon. I'll take the math book and do five more problems before Monday. Only five. That's it. I don't have to be crazy if I don't want to be. An obsessive can pick and choose among obsessions.

He put the suitcase back onto the unmade bed. He added a pair of hiking shorts and a sun-resistant Patagonia shirt he always wore in Willits. He closed the suitcase and went into the bathroom and got into the shower and closed his eyes and tried to think about the composition of water. Hydrogen, he was thinking. So much is invisible to us. We think we're so hot with our five senses but we know nothing, really. Ninety-nine percent of what is going on escapes us. Ninety-nine percent to the tenth power or the thousandth power. The rest we know. We are so wonderful in our egos, dressed out in all our ignorance and bliss. Our self-importance, our blessed hope.

Freddy went up a last long curve, cut off on a dirt road for half a mile, then stopped the Jeep at the foot of an abandoned gold mine. "Watch your step," he said to the girls. "There are loose stones everywhere. You have to keep an eye on the path. It's rough going all the way to where the trees begin."

"It's so nice here," Lydia said. "I feel like no one's been here in years. I bet we're the only people on this mountain. Do you think we are, Dad? Do you think anyone else is climbing it today?"

"I doubt it. Nieman and I never saw a soul when we were here. Of course, we have managed to keep our mouths shut about it, unlike some people who have to photograph and publish every good spot they find."

"Feel the air," Tammili added. "It tastes like spring. I'm glad we're here, Dad. This is a thousand times better than some old ski resort."

"Was a ski resort a possibility?" Freddy was trying not to grin.

"No. But some people went to them. Half the school went to Sun Valley. I don't care. I'd lots rather be in the wilderness with you."

"I'm glad you approve. Look up there. Not a cloud in the sky. What a lucky day."

"There's a cloud formation in the west," Tammili said. "I've been watching it for half an hour." They turned in the direction of the sea. Sure enough. On the very tip of the horizon a gray cloud was approaching. Nothing to worry about. Not a black system. Just a very small patch of gray on the horizon.

"Gather up the packs," Freddy said. "Let's start climbing. The sooner we make camp the sooner we don't have to worry about the weather. Those trees up there have withstood a thousand years of weather. We'd be safe there in a hurricane."

"What about a map check?" Tammili asked. She was pulling the straps of her pack onto her strong, skinny shoulders. Lydia was beside her, looking equally determined. This will never come again, Freddy thought. This time when they are children and women in the same skin. This innocence and power. My angels.

"Daddy. Come to." Lydia touched his sleeve, and he turned and kissed her on the head.

"Of course. Get a drink of water out of the thermos we're leaving. Then we'll climb up to that lookout and take our bearings." He handed paper cups to them and they poured water from a thermos and drank it, then folded the cups and left them in the Jeep. They hiked up half a mile to a lookout from where they could see the terrain between them and the place they were going. "Take a reading," Freddy said. "We'll write the readings down, but I want you to memorize them. Paper can get lost or wet. As long as the compass is on your wrist and you memorize the readings, you can find your way back to any base point."

"The best thing is to look where you're going," Tammili said. "Anyone can look at the sun and figure out where the ocean is."

"We won't always be hiking in Northern California," Freddy countered. "We'll do the Grand Canyon soon and then Nepal."

"Momma's friend Brittany got pregnant in Nepal," Lydia said. "She got pregnant with a monk. We saw pictures of the baby."

"Well, that isn't going to happen to either of you. I'm not going to let either of you get pregnant until you have an M.D. or a Ph.D., for starters. I may not let you get pregnant until you're forty. I was thinking thirty-five, now I'm thinking forty."

"We know. You're going to buy a freezer so we can freeze our eggs and save them until we can hire someone to have the babies." They started giggling again. When Lydia and Tammili decided something was funny, they thought it was funnier and funnier the more they laughed.

"Maps and compasses," Freddy said. "Find out where we are. Then find out where we're going, then chart a course."

"Where are we going?"

"Up there. To that cliff face. Around the corner is the waterfall that is the source of Red River." He watched as their faces bent toward their indescribably beautiful small wrists. The perfect bones and skin of ten-year-olds, burdened with the huge wrist compasses and watches. I could spend the day worshiping their arms, Freddy thought, or I could teach them something. "This is the Western Cordillera," he added. "Those are Douglas fir, as you know, and most of the others are pines, several varieties. Are the packs too heavy?"

"They're okay. We can stash things on the trail if we have to."

"In twenty minutes, we'll rest for five. All right?

"I think I hear the waterfall," he said. "Can you hear it?"

"Not if you're talking," Tammili said. "You have to be quiet to get nature to give up its secrets."

"Stop it, Tammili. Stop teasing him."

"Yeah, Tammili. Stop teasing me." They walked in silence then, up almost a thousand feet before they stopped to rest. The path was loose and slippery and the landscape to the east was barren and rough. To the west it was more dramatic. The cloud formation they had noticed earlier was growing into a larger mass.

"A gathering storm," Freddy said. "We'll be glad I put the waterproofing on the tent last night."

"I am glad," Lydia said. "I don't like to get wet when I'm camping."

"Let's go on then," Tammili said. "That might get here sooner than we think it's going to."

They shouldered the packs and began to climb again. Freddy was drawing the terrain in his mind. He had planned on camping at a site that was surrounded by watercourses. It was so steep that even if there was a deluge it would run off. Still, there was a dry riverbed that had to be crossed to get to the site. We could make for the caves, he was thinking. There wouldn't be bears this high but there are always snakes. Well, hell, I should have gotten a weather report but I didn't. That was stupid but we'll be safe.

"He's worrying," Tammili said to her sister.

"I knew he would. He thinks we'll get wet."

"I don't know about all this." Freddy stopped on the path above them and shook his head. "That cloud's worrying me. Maybe we should go back and camp by the Jeep. We could climb all around down there. We can go to Red River another time."

"We're halfway there," Tammili said. "We can't turn back now. We've got the tent. We'll get it up and if it rains, it rains."

"Yeah," Lydia agreed. "We'll ride it out."

In the solar-powered house Nora Jane was watching the sky. She would study for a while, then go outside and watch the weather. Finally, she started the old truck they kept for emergencies and tried to get a station on the radio. A scratchy AM station in Fort Bragg came on but it was only playing country music. She was about to drive the truck to town when she saw dust on the road and Nieman came driving up in his Volvo. "Thank God you came," she said, pulling open the door as soon as he parked. "Freddy took the girls to Red River and now it's going to storm. I could kill him for doing that. Why does he do such stupid things, Nieman? He didn't get a weather report and he just goes driving off to take the girls to see a waterfall."

"We'll go and find them," Nieman said. "Then we'll kill him. How about that?"

*   *   *

The adventurers climbed until they came to a dry riverbed that had to be crossed to gain the top. It was thirty feet wide and abruptly steep at the place where it could be crossed. The bed was a jumble of boulders rounded off by centuries of water. Some were as tall as a man. Others were the size of a man's head or foot or hand. Among the dark rounded boulders were sharper ones of a lighter color. "The sharp-looking pieces are granite," Freddy was saying. "It's rare in the coastal ranges. God knows where it was formed or what journeys it took to get here. Hang on to the large boulders and take your time. We are lucky it's dry. Nieman and I have crossed it when it's running, but I wouldn't let you." He led the girls halfway across the bed, then let them go in front of him, Tammili, then Lydia. They were surefooted and careful and he watched them negotiate the boulders with more than his usual pride. When they were across he started after them. A broken piece of granite caught his eye. He leaned over to pick it up. He stepped on a piece of moss and his foot slipped and kept on slipping. He stepped out wildly with his other foot to stop it. He kept on falling. He twisted his right ankle between two boulders and landed on his left elbow and shattered the humerus at the epicondyle.

"Don't come back here," he called. "Stay where you are. I'll crawl to you."

"Don't listen to him," Tammili said. She dropped her pack on the ground and climbed back over the boulders to where he lay gasping with pain. "Cut the pack strap," he said. "Use the big blade on your knife. Cut it off my shoulder if you can."

"What time did they leave?" Nieman asked. He had called the weather station and gotten a report and put in a preliminary request for information on distress flares in the area.

"They left about six-thirty this morning. Maybe they're on their way back. Freddy can see this front as well as we can. He wouldn't go up the mountain with a storm coming. All they have is that damned little tent. It barely sleeps three."

"They could go to the caves. I'm going to try to call him on the mobile phone. If they're driving, he'll answer." Nieman tried raising Freddy on the mobile phone, then called the telephone company and had them try. "Nothing. They can't get a thing. We are probably crazy to worry. What could go wrong? The girls are better campers than I am. They're not children."

"Tammili only weighs eighty pounds. I want to call the park rangers."

"Then call them. We'll tell them to be on the alert for flares from that area. I know he has flares with him. He loves flares. He always has them. Then we'll get in the Volvo and go look for them. I guess it will go down that road. Maybe we better take the truck."

"We have to make a stretcher and carry him to the trees," Tammili was saying. Freddy was slowly moving his body but he wasn't making much progress. He couldn't stand on his left ankle and he couldn't use his right arm and he could barely breathe for the pain. There were pain pills in the kit but he wouldn't take them. "At least I can think," he kept saying. "I can stand it and I can think. We have to get a shelter set up before the rain hits. I want you to go on over there and wait for me. I can make it. I'll get there." Then he went blank and the girls were standing over him.

"Let's go over to that stand of trees and tie down the supplies and get the tent cover and drag him on it," Tammili said. "If you start crying I'll smack you. What do you think we went to all those camps for? This is the emergency they trained us for. Come on. Help me drag his pack to the trees. Then we'll come back and get him. Nothing's going to happen to him. We can leave him for a minute."

They pulled Freddy's pack to the stand of pine trees where they had left their own. They tied the straps around a sapling and then found the tent cover and went back for him. The sky was very dark now but they did not notice it because they were ten years old and could live in the present.

They laid the tent cover down beside their father and tried to wake him. "You have to wake up and help us," Tammili was saying. "You have to roll over on the cover so we can drag it up the trail. Come on, Dad. It's going to rain. You'll get washed down the river. Come on. Move over here if you can." Freddy came to consciousness. He rolled over onto the tent cover with his left shoulder and tried to find a comfortable position. "Clear the rocks off the path," Lydia said. "Come on, Tammili. Let's clear the path." They began to throw the rocks to the side. Working steadily they managed to clear a way from the riverbed to the trees. Freddy lay on the cover with the pain coming and going like waves on the sea. He rocked in the pain. He let the pain take him. There was no way to escape it. Nora Jane will call for help, he was thinking. I know her. This is where her worrying will come in handy. The truck runs. She will drive it into town and call for help. The rain was beginning. He felt it on his face. Then the pain won and he didn't feel anything.

Lydia and Tammili came back down the path to the unconscious body of their father. They folded the tent cover around his body and began to pull him along the path they had cleared. Every two or three feet they would stop and try to wake him. Then they would scour the next few feet for branches and rocks. Then they would move him a few feet more. The rain was still falling softly, barely more than a mist. "It's good to get the ground wet," Tammili was saying. "It makes the tent slide."

"You aren't supposed to move wounded people. We could be making him worse."

"We aren't making him worse. His ankle's right there. We aren't moving it and his arm isn't moving. We're just going to that tree. We have to get away from the riverbed, Lydia. That thing could turn into a torrent. Keep pulling. Don't start crying. Nothing's going to happen. We're going to pull him to that tree and stay there until this storm is over."

"I don't believe this happened. How did it happen to us? We shouldn't have come up here."

"We only have a little more to go. Keep pulling. Don't talk so much." Tammili dug in her heels and pulled the weight of her father six more inches up and to the right of the path. Wind came around the side of the mountain and blew rain into their faces. She went to her father and pulled the tent cover more tightly around his body. She looked up at her sister. Their eyes met. Lydia was holding back her tears. "We only have one move," Tammili said. "We take the king to a place of safety. I'm a bishop and you're a rook. We're taking Dad to that tree, Lydia. We can do it if we will."

"I'm okay," Freddy said. "I can crawl up there. I'm okay, Lydia. Help me up, Tammili. This is just a rain. Just a rain that will end."

He half stood with Tammili supporting his side. He managed to hobble a few more feet in the direction of the tree. Lydia dragged the tent cover around in front of him and they laid him back down on it and pulled him the rest of the way.

Nora Jane and Nieman climbed into the Volvo and started across the property toward the old gold-mining road that Freddy and the girls had taken earlier that morning. "It's too low," Nieman said, after five minutes of driving. "It will never make it down that riverbed. Let's go back and get the truck."

"The truck barely runs."

"Well, we'll make it run."

"Let's call the ranger station again. I don't think we can overdo that. My God, Nieman, what's that noise?"

"I think it's a tire. It feels like something's wrong with a tire." He stopped the car and got out and stood looking at the left front tire. It was almost completely flat and getting flatter.

"You have a spare, don't you?" Nora Jane asked. She had gotten out and was standing beside him.

"No. I left it months ago to be repaired and never went back to pick it up. We'll have to walk back and get the truck."

"Call the ranger station first, then we'll get the truck." Nieman didn't argue. He got the ranger station on the phone. "No, we don't know they're lost. We just know they didn't know this weather was coming. You can put it in the computer, can't you? So if anyone sees a warning flare in that area they'll report it? He always has flares. . . . Because I know. Because I've been camping with him a hundred times. . . . Okay. Just so you're on the alert. We're going there now. It's the old gold-mining camp below Red River Falls. The waterfall that is the source of Red River. Surely you have it on a map. . . . All right. Thanks again. Thank you."

"Insanity. Bureaucrazy. Okay, my darling Nora Jane, let's get out and walk."

Halfway to the house it began to rain. By the time they reached the house they were soaking wet. They changed into dry clothes and got into the truck and started driving. This time they didn't talk. They didn't curse. They didn't plan. They just moved as fast as they could go in the direction of the people that they loved.

Tammili and Lydia had managed to drag Freddy almost to the tree. There was a reasonably flat patch of ground there and they surveyed it. "Let's put the tent up over him," Lydia suggested.

"We'd have to move him twice to do that. We haven't got time and besides we shouldn't move him any more than we have to."

"So what are we going to do?"

"We'll cover up with the tent and put all the packs and some rocks around to hold it down."

"Water's going to run in."

"Not if we fix it right. Get it out." Tammili was pulling things out of the packs. "We'll get him covered up, then I'll set off flares."

"You better set them off before it rains any more."

"Then hurry." They dragged the tent over to their father and draped it over his body. Lydia took the cape and wrapped it around his legs and feet. They pulled the tent cover up to make a rain sluice and set rocks against it to hold it in place.

"Finish up," Tammili said. "I'm going over there by the river-bed and set off flares." She had found a pack of them in the bottom of Freddy's pack. She pulled it out and read the directions. "Keep out of the hands of children. This is not a toy. Approved by the Federal Communications Commission and the Federal Bureau of Standards. Remove plastic cap carefully. Point in the direction of clear sky. Da. Pull down lever with a firm grasp. If three pulls does not release flare, discard and try another flare. Okay, here goes." She walked over to the cleared place. She pulled the lever down and a huge point of light rose to the sky and spread out and held.

"Do some more," Lydia called to her. Tammili set off four more flares. Then waited. Then set off two more. Rain was beginning to fall in earnest now. She went back to the pack and put the leftover flares where she had found them. Then she buckled up the pack and put the smaller packs on top of it. Then she dragged the synchilla blanket underneath the tent and she and Lydia lay down on each side of their father. The rain was falling harder. They arranged the synchilla blanket over Freddy's body and then covered that with the cape. They found each other's hands. The fingers of Lydia's right hand fit into the fingers of Tammili's left hand as they had always done.

A volunteer fire lookout worker was in a fire tower ten miles from where they lay covered with the cape and tent. He was a twenty-year-old student who had always been good at every-thing he did. He prided himself on being good at things. Every other Thursday when he spent his three hours in the tower he was on the lookout every second. He didn't go down and fill his coffee cup. He didn't read books. He kept his eyes on the sky and the land. That was what he had volunteered to do and that is what he did. Earlier, before he began his stint, he had pulled up all the local data on a computer and read it carefully. He had especially noted the memo about Red River because his mother was a geologist and had taken him there as a child. He saw the first flare out of the corner of his eye just as it was dying. He saw the second and the third and fourth flares, but lost the last two in the approaching storm. "I will be damned," he decreed. "I finally saw something. It finally paid off to stay alert." He called the ranger station and reported what he had seen.

Nora Jane and Nieman were driving the four miles of rocky trail between blacktop and blacktop. They were driving in a blinding rain. Nieman was at the wheel. Nora Jane was pushing back into the seat imagining her life without her husband and her daugh-ters. I don't know why we built that crazy house to begin with, Nieman was thinking. I hate it there. Grass doesn't grow. You can't take a hot shower half the time. It's a dangerous place. We should have been down in the inner city building houses for people to live in. Not some goddamn, lonely, scary, dangerous trap on a barren hillside. He shouldn't have taken them up there, much less to Red River. As though they are expendable. As though we could ever breathe again if anything happened to them. But what could happen? Nothing will happen. They'll get wet, then we'll get them dry. He steered the old red truck down onto the blacktop and pushed the pedal to the floor. "I'm gunning it," he said to Nora Jane. "Hold on."

"Don't worry, Daddy," Tammili was crooning. "Momma will send someone to get us. Remember when Lydia broke her arm and it got all right. Her hand was hanging off her wrist like nothing and it grew back fine."

"It sure did," Lydia said. "It grew right back."

"Get behind the rocks," Freddy said. "Don't stay here. I'm okay. I'm doing fine." A sheet of lightning blazed a mile away. It seemed to be beside them. "It's okay," Freddy said. "Cuddle up. Rain always stops. It always stops. It always does."

"Sometimes it rains for two days," Lydia put in. She snuggled down into a ball beside her father. She patted her father's chest. She patted his ribs. She patted his heart. Another burst of lightning flashed even closer. Then the rain began to fall twice as hard as it had before. The earth seemed to sink beneath the force of the rain, but they were warm beneath the cape and the tent and they were together.

"These are Franciscan rocks," Tammili said. "The whole Coast Range is made up of the softest, weirdest rocks they know. Geologists don't know what they are. They used to be the ocean floor. Where we are, right now, as high as it seems, used to be stuff on the floor of the ocean."

"That's right," Lydia added. "Before that it was the molten center of the earth."

"The continents ride on the seas like patches of weeds in a marsh," Tammili went on. "Fortunately for us it all moves so slowly that we'll be dead before it changes enough to matter. Unless the big earthquake puts it all back in the sea."

"Who told you that?" Freddy tried to rise up on his good arm. The pain in the other one had subsided for a moment. He was

beginning to be able to move his foot. "When the storm sub-
sides we'll put up the rest of the flares. They'll be looking for
us. Someone's looking for us now."

"We could drive the car," Lydia whispered. A third network
of lightning had covered the mountain with clear blue light. Far
away the thunder rumbled, but the lightning seemed to be only
feet away. "One of us could stay with you and the other one
could get in the Jeep and go for help."

"They'll find us," Freddy said. "Your mother will be right on
top of this. If we don't come back, she'll send for help." The rain
was harder now, beating on the flattened tent. Still, they seemed
to be warm and dry. "This cape wicks faster than synchilla,"
Freddy added. "Just like Nieman to find this and leave it lying
around." The pain returned full force then and Freddy felt
himself going down. Don't think, he told himself. Turn it off.
Don't let it in.

"Hold my hand," Lydia said and reached for her sister. "Tell
more about the coast and the ocean. Tell the stuff Nieman tells
us."

"It was a deep trench, the whole coast, the whole state of
California. And the ocean and the hot middle of the earth keep
churning and pushing and hot stuff comes up from the middle,
like melted fire, only more like hot, hot honey, and it's very
beautiful and red and gold and finally it turns into rocks and
mud and gets pushed up to make mountains. Then the trench
got filled with stuff and it rose up like islands and made California. Then the Great Plains got in the middle of the Coast
Range and the Sierra Nevada and the Cascades. They are real
thick mountains and all crystallized together with granite. But
not the Coast Range. The Coast Range is made of strange rocks
and there is jade left here by serpentine. And maganese and
mercury and bluechist and gold and everything you could want."

"Serpentinite," Freddy said. "Manganese."

Nieman was saying, "You stay in the truck and wait for the
rangers. Work on the phone in Freddy's Jeep. You might get it
working. I'm going up."

They were standing at the base of the path. It was still

pouring rain. Nieman was wearing a foul-weather parka and was laden with signal devices, everything they had found in the house and cars.

"Go on then. Start climbing. I'll do what I can."

"Do whatever you decide to do." He looked at her then, this beautiful, whimsical creature whom his best friend adored, and he understood the adoration as never before. Her whole world was in danger and she was breathing normally and was not whining. Nieman gave her a kiss on the cheek and turned and began to climb. The rain was coming down so fast it was difficult to see, but he knew the path and he was careful. Maybe we should have gone for help instead of coming here. Maybe we should have done a dozen things. The rangers know. Surely to God they are on their way.

The ranger helicopter had turned back from the lightning and now a truck carrying a medic was headed in their direction but the road had been washed out in two places and they had had to ford it. "Plot the coordinates of the flares again," the driver said. "Are you sure twenty-four is the nearest road?"

"There's an old creek bed we might navigate, but not in this weather. An old mining road leads to within a mile. I'd rather take that. Here, you look at the map."

"Jesus, what a storm. A frog strangler, that's what we call them where I come from."

"Two little girls and their father. I'd like to kill some people. What the hell does a man want to go off for with kids this far from nowhere? It kills me. I used to teach wilderness safety at the hospital. What a waste of breath."

"Land of the free. Home of the foolhardy. Okay, I think I can make it across that water. Let's give it a try." He drove the vehicle across a creek and made it to the other side. As soon as they were across, the medic put on his seat belt and pulled it down tight across his waist and chest.

"Four hundred and three," Nieman was counting. "Four hundred and four. Four hundred and five."

*   *   *

Nora Jane sat in the passenger seat of the Jeep and worked on the phone. Once or twice she was able to hear static and she kept on trying. She took the batteries out and wiped them on her shirt and put them back in. She moved every movable part. She prayed to her old Roman Catholic God. She prayed to Mary. She made promises.

The storm was moving very slowly across the chaos of disordered rocks that is the Coast Range of Northern California. The birds pulled their wings over their heads. The panthers dreamed in their lairs. The scraggly vegetation drank the water as fast as it fell. When the sun came back out it would use the water to grow ten times as fast as vegetation in wetter climates. Tammili and Lydia held hands. Freddy slept. An infinitesimal part of the energy we call time became what we call history.

"Six thousand and one," Nieman counted. He wanted to stop and wipe his glasses but he could not bring himself to waste a second. Some terrible intuition led him on. Some danger or unease that had bothered him ever since the night before. He had come to where he was needed. It was not the first time that had happened to him. That's why I hated those movies, he told himself. When no one believed what they knew. When no one learned anything. The beginning of *Karate Kid* was okay. The beginning of it was grand.

He had come to a creek bed that was now a torrent of rushing water. I know this, he remembered. But how the hell will I cross it now? He stood up straight. He pushed the hood back from his parka and reached for his glasses to wipe them. A huge bolt of lightning shook the sky. It illuminated everything in sight. By its light Nieman saw the pile of tent and figures on the ground on the other side of the water. "Freddy," he screamed at the top of his lungs. "It's me. It's Nieman. Freddy, is that you?"

The rest was drowned by thunder. Then Nieman saw a small figure rise up from the pile. She came out from under the tent and began waving her hands in the air.

"I'll get there," he yelled. "Stay where you are." The rain was slacking somewhat. Nieman found a flat place a few yards down the creek and began to make his way across the rocks. Lydia met him on the other side. "Dad's broken his arm and foot," she told him. "We need to get him to a doctor."

The medic spotted the Jeep and the truck. "There they are," he yelled at the driver. "There're the fools. Let's go get them."

An hour later Freddy was on a stretcher being brought down the mountain by four men. The clearing was filled with vehicles. The brown cape was thrown into the back of an EMS van. It would end up at the city laundry. Then on the bed of a seven-year-old Mexican girl who had been taken from her mother. But that is another story.

Ten days later a party gathered at Chez Panisse to eat an early dinner and discuss the events of the past week. There were nine people gathered at Freddy Harwood's favorite table by the window in the back room. The young man who had seen the flares, the medic, the driver, Nieman, Freddy, Nora Jane, Tammili, Lydia, and a woman biochemist who was after Nieman to marry him. Her name was Stella Light and this was the first time Nieman had taken her out among his friends. It was the first time he had taken her to Chez Panisse and the first time he had introduced her to Nora Jane and Freddy and the twins. Stella Light was dressed in her best clothes, a five-year-old gray pant-suit and a white cotton blouse. She had almost added a yellow scarf but had taken it off minutes after she put it on.

"We had this magic cape we found under the bed," Lydia was telling her. "The minute we say something's magic, it is magic, that's what Uncle Nieman says. It's probably his cape but he can't remember it. He leaves his stuff everywhere. Did you know that? He's absentminded because he is a genius. Do you go to school with him? Is that how you met him?"

"Well, I teach in the department. Tell me about the cape."

"It kept us warm. Dad thinks it was synchilla. Anyway, it was raining so hard it felt like rocks were falling on us."

"It was lightning like crazy," Tammili added. "There was light-ning so near it made halos around the trees."

"Tammili!" Freddy shook his head.

"You don't know. You were incoherent from pain."

"Incoherent?" Stella laughed.

"She always talks like that," Lydia said. "It's Uncle Nieman. He's been working on our vocabularies since we were born."

"I'm having goat cheese pie and salad," Nieman said. "I think he wants to take our orders. Menus up, ladies. Magic cape, my eye. Magic forest rangers and volunteer distress signal watchers." He stood up and raised his glass to the medic and the driver and the young man. "To your honor, gentlemen. We salute thee."

"To all of us," Freddy added, raising his glass with his good hand. "My saviors, my family, my friends."

Nieman caught Stella's eye as they drank. A long sweet look that was not lost on Tammili and Lydia. We could be the bridesmaids, Lydia decided. We never get to be in weddings. None of Mom and Dad's friends ever get married. Pretty soon we'll be too old to be bridesmaids. It will be too late.

"Stop it," Tammili whispered to her sister, pretending to be bending over to pick up a napkin so she wouldn't be scolded for telling secrets at the table. "Stop wanting that woman to marry Uncle Nieman. Uncle Nieman doesn't need a girlfriend. He's got everything he needs. He's got Mom and Dad and you and me." When she sat up she batted her eyes at her godfather. Then, for good measure, she got up and walked around the table and gave him a hug and stood by his side. Oh, my God, Stella was thinking. Well, that's an obstacle that can be overcome. Children are such little beasts nowadays. It makes you want to get your tubes tied.

"Go back to your chair," Nora Jane said to her daughter. "Let Uncle Nieman eat his goat cheese pie."

The Affair

Nieman Gluuk was finally going to be taken to bed. Not that he hadn't had love affairs before. He had had them but they hadn't meant to him what they mean to most of us. They hadn't thrown him to the mat. They hadn't given him a taste of what men kill and die for, dream about. One Stella Light of Salem, Oregon, was going to be the one to do it. Thirty-seven years old, five feet six inches tall, dark haired and dark eyed, a physicist, a biochemist, and a distance runner. A control freak. An expert on viral diseases of poultry. The only child of a high school science teacher and a librarian. A small-breasted woman who had dyed her hair platinum blond the week before she met Nieman and begun wearing a devastatingly expensive perfume called Joy. Her clock was ticking and her hours staring at photographs taken by electron microscopes had not given her any reason to put off doing anything she wanted to do.

It is dawn. Stella gets up and makes the bed. She puts on a white T-shirt and a pair of cutoff blue jeans and some high-tech Nike running shoes. She rubs sunblock lotion on her arms and face. She pours a cup of coffee that was made automatically at five o'clock by her combination clock radio and coffeemaker.

She walks out onto her porch. She surveys the mist that has

come in the night before. She imagines the coast of California
swaying on its shaky underpinnings. She goes down the stairs
and begins to run. In five minutes the endorphins kick in. In
five minutes the blood is in her legs instead of her cerebral
cortex, and for the only time during the day she is free of
thinking, thinking, thinking.

She runs uphill for a mile, then cuts over to the Berkeley
campus. She runs the length of the campus three times, back
and forth, and back again. She stops once to pick up a curled
leaf that has fallen from a tree. It has been infested with a bole.
She scratches the bole open and squints at it, then puts it in
the pocket of her shorts. She has been inspecting leaves since
she was three years old.

Nothing surprises Stella. And everything interests her. Of
late, she has found herself musing on reproduction more than
she thinks is healthy. Leaf, bole, tree, nuts, seeds, eggs. Not to
mention the terrible viral splittings on the screens of the microscopes. As Stella runs through the campus she forces her
mind to stay in the realm of vertebrates. I should use one of my
eggs, her mind keeps repeating. No one else carries Grandfather
Bass's genes. No one else carries Mother's or Aunt Georgia's. I
am the last. I should go deeper into life. Life is dangerous and
awful. Still, it is all we have. I am tired of being perfect. Perhaps
I am tired of being alone. Perhaps this is true. Perhaps it is a
trick the hormones play.

Nieman had been laid before. He had slept with prostitutes and
he had slept with a girl from Ohio for five months in 1973. He
had slept with a French girl one summer when he and Freddy
went to study French at the Sorbonne. What he had not done
was fall in love. All he had seen around him were the ruins of
love. His parents' marriage had been a disaster. He barely knew
his father. The hundreds of movies he had reviewed and all the
books he had read taught him that love was a wasteland, a
tornado, an earthquake, a fire. Men and women in love were like
children, given over to childlike jealousies and self-loathing and
despair.

*   *   *

When he ran into Stella late one afternoon as they were both leaving the biochemistry building and knocked her papers out of her hand, he had no idea that his life was being changed. He had a premonition, a terrible sense of déjà vu, and so did she, but Nieman thought it was the weather and Stella thought it was because she was about to begin her period.

"They weren't numbered," she said, as she knelt to pick up the papers. "Well, that's not your fault, is it?"

"Oh, God, oh, please let me pick them up. Don't do that. I'm so sorry. Let me help you?"

"Have we met?" She was kneeling only feet away from him. She was wearing a blue denim skirt, a soft blue shirt, little blue sneakers like you see on sale at the grocery store. She smelled of some heavenly perfume, some odor of divinity. Underneath the shirt was a soft white camisole with lace along the edges. In the center of the camisole was a small pink flower. "I'm having a déjà vu," she added. "It's such an odd sensation. I'm probably hungry. I get crazy when I don't eat. Blood sugar. Oh, well."

"That's dangerous. Let me feed you. Please. Come with me." He had gathered up the rest of the papers. He stood up. He took her hand and pulled her up beside him. "Please. Come have dinner with me. I'll help you straighten up the papers. I'm hungry too."

"Well, if you'll go someplace near. How about the Grill across from the library?"

"Great. I like it there. I go there all the time. I'm Nieman Gluuk. I'm a student."

"I know who you are. You're the talk of the department. Did you really quit the paper to study science?"

"I wish that story hadn't gotten out. I'm a neophyte. A bare beginner. It's pitiful how far I have to go."

"Oh, I doubt that."

Twenty minutes later they were sitting in a booth at the Grill eating French fries and waiting for their omelets. They were telling each other the stories of their lives.

"So when they quit the Merry Pranksters, they moved back to Salem and had me. They were worried they had fucked up their DNA with all the acid they had done so they had me tested all the time. It turned out I test well. Then they decided I'm a genius. I'm not. I just learned to take the tests. So, out of their relief that I wasn't an idiot, they turned into the worst bourgeois you can imagine. They collect furniture. You wouldn't believe the furniture my mom can cram into a room. Danish modern, English antiques . . . Anyway, I like them. They leave me alone, considering I'm an only child. They work for environmental groups and they have a lot of friends. They're pretty people. Both of them are a lot prettier than I am. I look like my maternal grandfather, who invented dental floss, by the way. He was a dentist in New Orleans."

"You're very pretty. You're as pretty as you can be. You don't think you're pretty?"

"I'm okay. You ought to see them. They look like early-retirement poster people. So, what set of events made you?"

"An undependable father and an unhappy mother. No wonder I started going to the movies. She's a frustrated actress. I grew up thinking the theater was real life."

"Well, I'm a fan. I always read your column. I loved the things you wrote. I can't believe you just quit doing it."

"Twenty years. It got so unpleasant at the end. I couldn't please anyone. Even people I praised didn't think the praise went far enough. Now I want to know the rest. The things you know. I can't wait to use an electron microscope."

"They haven't let you use it?"

"They were supposed to last week, then the class was canceled."

"Oh, I know what happened. The Benning-Rohrer was down and we had to double up on the SEM. I'll show them to you. We can go there after dinner if you like."

The waiter appeared and put plates of steaming omelets in front of them. This is not what I thought would happen, Nieman was thinking. Always what you least expect. I already feel the air getting thin. Freddy told me someday this would happen to me but I thought he was projecting.

Look at that forebrain, Stella was thinking. The cerebral cortex. The verbal skills. I could breed with that, if I am being driven to breed. She sat very still. She picked at her food. She lifted a hand and touched her mouth with her finger.

"Are you left-handed?" Nieman asked.

"Yes."

"I am too."

When they had finished eating they walked back across the campus to the biochemistry building and went up to Stella's office and left the papers, which they had forgotten to put in order, on her desk. Then they went into the laboratory and sat down in the chairs before the scanning electron microscope.

"How much do you know?" Stella asked.

"'The scanning electron microscope . . . a beam of electrons is scanned over the surface of a solid object and used to build up an image of the details of the surface structure. There are also several special types of electron microscope. Among the most valuable is the electron-probe microanalyzer, which allows a chemical analysis of the composition of materials to be made by using the incident electron beam to excite the emission of characteristic X radiation by the various elements composing the specimen. These X rays are detected and analyzed by spectrometers built into the instrument. Such probe microanalyzers are able to produce an electron-scanning image so that structure and composition may be easily correlated.'"

"My heavens. How did you do that?"

"My brand-new Encyclopedia Britannica, Macropaedia, volume twenty-four, page sixty-six. Do you want more?" Nieman was leaned back in the chair. He was smiling. He was almost laughing. He was wearing thin khaki pants. His legs were strong and spread out on the chair.

"Go on."

"'Fundamental research by many physicists in the first quarter of the twentieth century suggested that cathode rays (i.e., electrons) might be used in some way to increase microscopic resolution. Louis de Broglie, a French physicist, in 1924 opened the way with the suggestion that electron beams might be regarded as a form of wave motion. De Broglie derived the formula for their wavelength, which showed, for example, that, for electrons accelerated by sixty-thousand volts, the effective wavelength . . .' What? Why are you laughing?"

"Photographic memory?"

"Of course. It's selective, and I have to be interested in something to imprint it. I've seen movies I can't remember at all. That was a test. If I couldn't remember them, I didn't review them."

Stella was looking at his pants. He sat up straighter in the chair. He pulled his legs together. He coughed. "'The electron image must be made visible to the eye by allowing the electrons to fall on a fluorescent screen. Such a screen is satisfactory for quick observations and for focusing and aligning the instrument. A low-power binocular optical microscope fitted outside the column allows the flower on the screen, I mean the image on the screen, to be inspected at a magnification of about ten magnitudes. . . .'"

"You want to see the AIDS virus?" Stella asked. She pulled a box of slides from a drawer and inserted one into a locked compartment at the base of the instrument. "This is the virus on a human T-cell. I really hate this slide." She pushed a button and the lights came on the screen. Then an image appeared. Long tubular cells covered with watery stars of death.

"I've been to one hundred and seven funerals since this thing started," Nieman said. "Have you been tested?"

"Dozens of times. This job has its drawbacks. I essentially hate viruses. I'm not one of those biologists who love nature. Nature is not on our side. It's always trying to take us back. I'm for the higher mammals straight out. How about you? Have you been tested?"

"My dentist tested me. He never called me back so I assumed I was all right. How accurate do you think the tests are?" Nieman leaned forward to study the screen. It was terrible to behold. "Cut it off," he said and went back to looking at the flower in the center of the camisole under Stella's blouse.

Stella pressed a button. The screen went blank. The room was quiet. The overwhelming sense of déjà vu returned.

"I keep thinking I've been here before," Nieman said. "In this room with you. It's the damnedest thing."

"I feel it too," she answered. "I'm thirty-seven. I keep thinking about breeding. It's probably hormonal. We are primates, don't forget that." She turned around on the swivel chair and looked at him.

"Should we resign ourselves to that?"

"We could welcome it."

"You think so?" Nieman stood up. "There it is again," he said. "It's the damnedest thing. Déjà vu, it means *already seen*. Of course we must have met somewhere. Then, of course, the gene pool is wide. These things might be chemical. See, I'm beginning to think like one of you." He smiled down at her and she reached up and touched, first his sleeve, then his hand. She didn't take his hand or grab it. She brushed her fingers across the back of his hand, then left them only inches away from him. "I don't have much experience with women, sexually, that is." Nieman kept on smiling at her and at himself, at the strangeness of the moment, the silliness and divinity of it. "But I haven't given up on myself. I'd like to have an affair with someone, something that mattered, that might matter to them also. Am I out of line here? You can hit me or dismiss me."

"I haven't had a lover in three years. If I had a love affair I'd be the inexperienced one. I always start thinking what I'm doing is funny. Not the sexual part, per se, you know, but the thing entire, as it were. Well, what are we talking about here?"

"I think we are saying we like each other more than ordinary. I am saying that. I am saying, would you imagine some day, in your time, on your terms, having me as a candidate for a lover?"

"We could get an AIDS test in the morning and have the results back in a day. Then, if we still wanted to, we could explore this further. I have some time after my nine o'clock class." She went on and put her hands on his hands. "I'll admit this is partly about your verbal skills."

"For me it's the flower on your undershirt and your Ph.D." Nieman laughed. "Or the electrical systems in this building are affecting our brains. Tell me where to meet you. I'll be there."

"Would we really do this?"

"I think we are doing it. In my old life I always maintained that thought was action. So the question is: Would we actually carry it out?"

"It's what the young people do, but not the first time they knock the papers out of someone's hands."

"How long do they wait?"

"I think three days. I heard three days from someone who was confessing something to me. I'm a student adviser part time."

"Then grown people only have to wait one day because we have a shorter time to live."

"That's a theory? Shall we leave now?"

"I suppose we should. Let me help you turn things off."

"All right. The switches are on the wall." They turned off the lights in the laboratory and walked to the elevator holding hands. They went down on the elevator and Nieman walked her to her car. "What time in the morning?" he asked.

"You're serious?"

"More than I've ever been in my life."

"Do you know where the student health center is now?"

"Yes."

"Meet me there at quarter past ten." It was very still in the tree-bordered parking lot. The earth smelled like birth and death and love. There were stars in the sky and a new moon above the physics building. Luckily they were both intuitive, feeling types. A sensate might have swooned.

At ten-fifteen the next morning they met at the student health center and asked to be tested for the AIDS virus. They filled out forms and sat in the waiting room reading magazines and were called in and blood was drawn and the nurse told them to call that afternoon for the results. "Sometimes it takes a couple of days if they're backed up but it's been slow this week. I'll tell them it's for you, Doctor Light. I think you'll get these back by five." She smiled a professional smile and Nieman held open the door for Stella and they walked back out into the waiting room and out the door onto the blooming spring campus. "Are you free tomorrow?" he asked.

"Pretty much. I have some papers to grade."

"I was thinking we could drive up Highway One to Mendo-cino and spend the weekend together. I mean, no matter how the tests come out. I want to talk to you. I want to be with you some more. I don't know how to say all this."

"I would love to go to Mendocino with you."

"Will you have dinner with me tonight?"

"Yes. Yes I will."

"I don't know where you live."

"Then you'll find out, won't you? Call me at six. If we're positive, we'll get drunk. If we're negative, we'll, I don't know."

"We'll be negative. Perhaps all we are supposed to do about that is be grateful. I'll call then. I'll call at six."

A young technician named Alice Yount put the slides under-neath the microscope and watched the fine, free T-cells swim in their sea. She called the health center and made the report and then sent the papers over. It was a good morning. Only one test had come back positive and that was a man who had known it already. Some happiness, Alice was thinking as she took off her apron and washed her hands. Some good news.

At seven o'clock that night Nieman appeared at Stella's door. He was wearing a blue shirt he bought in Paris. He was wearing his best silk socks and seersucker pants and he had taken off his watch and ring. I am putting myself in the path of pain and suffering and life, he told himself. I am a Mayan sacrifice. I have seen this movie but I have never played in it. I can't believe it is this exciting and terrible and irresistible. I want to burn every word I've ever written. What did I know?

Then she was there and they walked into her kitchen and poured glasses of water and sipped them and were shy. They walked around her house looking at the books, the bare stone floors, the clean windows, the stark white walls, the wide white bed.

It was not silly when it happened and neither of them was afraid. "Nice scar," he told her later, examining her knee.

"Bike wreck when I was ten," she answered. "What do you have to show me?"

"Navel?" he asked. "Appendix scar? Cut on eyebrow?"

At two in the morning Nieman went home to pack for the weekend. "I forgot my sleeping pills," he explained. "There are limits to what the psyche can take. I might keep you up all night."

"Go on," she answered. "We're pushing the envelope. I'd like to be alone for a few hours. What do you take?"

"Ambien. Benadryl. Xanax if I travel. If I'm at home I usually just stay awake."

"Distressing, all the people who can't sleep. Do you think it's the modern world?"

"No. I think it's always been that way. Neurotic from the start. That's how I view our history. Short lived and neurotic. Now we're long lived and neurotic. I call that progress, any way you look at it."

"Me too."

At ten the next morning Nieman picked her up in Freddy Harwood's Jeep Cherokee and they drove out over the Golden Gate Bridge and took the Stinson Beach exit and began the 1,500-foot climb into the coastal hills. At Muir Woods they got out of the car and held hands and looked at the ocean for a long time. Already their bodies were joined at the hip. Already there was nothing that could keep them apart.

"Where's Nieman?" Nora Jane was asking. "What did he want the Cherokee for?"

"I think he's in love," Freddy answered. "It's the damnedest thing you've ever seen. He's trying to keep it a secret."

"Who is she?"

"I don't know. He wouldn't even look at me."

"He's getting laid. My God, imagine that."

"He had on a brand-new polo shirt."

"You're kidding."

"I am not. May lightning strike me if I am. It still had the creases in it. He hadn't even washed it."

"My folks drove this highway on the bus," Stella was saying. "I wish they didn't disavow that so much. They were just kids. Everything is in a state of anarchy, Nieman. Every single thing we see about us. Our universe is a nanosecond, the blink of an eyelash, and yet, we are here and this experience seems vast. Last night, after you left, I fell asleep giggling. I kept seeing us marching into the student health center to be tested. That will be all over the campus by the time we get back. Technically I can't date you, you know. Since you are a student."

"We aren't dating." Nieman slowed down. He drove the car to a wide place that overlooked the sea. He turned off the motor and turned to her and took her hands. "I am in love with you. That's been clear since Friday afternoon at six o'clock. I have waited all my life for you. I want to marry you, or live with you, or do whatever you want to do. I have three hundred and forty-seven thousand dollars in assets and no responsibilities I can't get rid of in an hour. I will go anywhere you want to go. I will live any life you want to live."

"My goodness."

"I wrote that down several times this morning. There's a draft of it in my jacket pocket. You can have it."

"Let's get something to eat first. I can't get engaged on an empty stomach."

"This is real, Stella. This is deadly serious on my part."

"I know that. I'm serious too. Don't you think I know a miracle when one slaps me in the face?" Then Nieman was extremely glad he had borrowed Freddy's Cherokee, because it had an old-fashioned front seat and Stella slid over next to him and stayed there all the way to Stinson Beach.

Which is how Tammili and Lydia Harwood finally got to be bridesmaids in a wedding. "I thought it would never happen," Lydia told her friends. "The last person I thought would give us this window of opportunity was Uncle Nieman. I am wearing pink."

"And I am wearing blue," Tammili would add. "It's going to be at our beach house. There will be two cakes and lots of petits fours and Jon Ragel from *Vogue* is going to take the photographs."

"Uncle Nieman will never get a Nobel now," Lydia would sigh. "Dad says Nieman has forgotten all about wanting a Nobel prize for biochemistry."

Design

GABRIELA WAS FIRST in line when the truck from the Salvation Army pulled into the driveway of the orphanage and unloaded the boxes. The older girls tore open the first box and began to sort through the clothes. The nun who was in charge had gone inside to finish a book she was reading.

Gabriela was only seven years old but even the older girls wouldn't tangle with her. She had come to the orphanage three months before and quickly established a reputation as a dangerous adversary. She would kick and bite and never back down. Also, she had an ally. An enormous eleven-year-old named Annie who had red hair and was listed as an incorrigible. An incorrigible was the best thing you could be at Santa Ramona del Rio in Potrero. Even the nuns didn't cross the incorrigibles.

Gabriela let the older girls open the first two boxes. Then she went up to the third box and tore it open and took the first garment in the pile. At first she thought it was a blanket but when she shook it out she saw it was a cape. A long brown cape of some very soft, very fine material. She threw it over her shoulders and walked off down the long covered walkway to her room. She took the cape into the room and laid it across the bed. Something about it appealed to her. It reminded her of a lighter, warmer world. Not the house with many children where the food was nasty. Not the thin man with the ugly nose. Not the time before that in the truck. Someplace that was warm and sunny, where women with soft bosoms were laughing in the sun. Gabriela lay down upon the cape and wrapped the edges around her arms and fell asleep. It was Saturday morning. There was nothing she had to do until noon, when the bells would ring to call her in to lunch.

"They want a little girl. Someone who needs a family," the social worker from Oklahoma was saying on the phone to Sister Maria Rebecca. "They lost their child in an accident. They're fine people. Good, stable, attractive people. They speak Spanish, although the child would need some English to start school. Any age. Their child was four. They told me in Los Angeles you had the ones no one else will take."

"We have seventy girls," Sister Maria Rebecca answered. "Perhaps they would like to come and see them."

"They want a child who needs them. Someone you can't place elsewhere. Anyone in Oklahoma City will vouch for them. They're devout. There wouldn't be a problem with that."

"I might know the child for them," Sister Maria Rebecca said. "Yes, there is one I was worrying about this morning. She bit the last two people who tried to keep her."

"I know this couple personally. She's capable and kind. They could come any time."

"They have to understand we can't guarantee adoption. We don't know where she came from. She's been in the system two years since she was abandoned in San Diego. She's a pretty little thing, healthy and strong. Yes, they should come and meet her. We call her Gabriela."

"I'm sure they'll come soon. They're determined about this. They're not looking for a child to save them, you know, they just want to be of use."

"Send them on. I will look forward to talking to them."

That was Saturday morning. On Saturday afternoon, the social worker, whose name was Denise, got into her car and drove over to Allen and Jennifer Williams's house and got out and walked up the path to the door. Jennifer was on her knees by a bed of flowers. She got up when she saw Denise and walked toward her. She pulled off a yellow glove and used the free hand to shove her hair out of her face. She was a beautiful woman. Even in sweat pants and an old shirt. Even with grief written on her face as if forever. "What's happened?" she asked. "Could you find out anything?"

"There's a place in California that has children no one wants. The sister who runs it said there's a child you can meet. A little girl. Are you sure you want to do this, Jennifer?"

"Yes. I have to be of use in some simple, clear way. Just to feed and dress a child. Keep it safe. Nothing more complicated than that."

She pulled off the second glove and put them in the pocket of the pants. "Come inside. Tell us what you know."

They found Allen Williams in the kitchen. There were untouched newspapers on a table. He was sitting beside them looking out the window. It was very quiet in the house. Everything was in its place. No disorder anywhere. Not a sound.

"I should have called," Denise said. "But I wanted to see your faces. There's a little girl in California you can meet. This is going to be expensive, Allen. Are you sure you're up for this?"

"There's plenty of money." Allen got up and held out a chair for her. "We can go whenever you want us to go."

"How about Monday?"

"Monday's fine. The office doesn't care. They'll do anything to help."

"It could be a wild goose chase. It's a home for girls they don't know what to do with. They don't have records for some of them. And it wouldn't be a final adoption. Maybe couldn't ever be one. You'd just be volunteering to be out-of-state foster parents. I don't think there's a chance of losing one of these children once you have one, though. It's never happened. I researched this for days, Allen. Several people I trust told me about this place. The child would be healthy and free of disease. That's about all I could guarantee."

"We'll go." Jennifer came around and sat beside Denise. "Thank you for this. For all this trouble. You don't know what it means, to have this hope."

"You may not thank me a month from now."

"We're going to do this," Allen said. "And we're going to see it through. If we bring a child up here we'll keep her no matter what. My brother's a child psychiatrist. Our parents know."

"Allen said if all else failed he'd teach the child to ride," Jennifer said. "He says we'll move to the country if we have to and be cowboys."

"Okay." Denise opened her briefcase and got out a sheet of paper. "Get the airlines on the phone. Here's where we're going. I'll go with you if you want."

"We can do it." Allen took the paper from her and began to dial the phone. "If we need you, we'll call and you can come out later."

Jennifer put her hand on Denise's shoulder. The refrigerator began to hum. A child's drawing on the refrigerator door moved in the breeze from the air-conditioning vent. It was a drawing of a house. There was a setting sun. A moon, some stars, a cloud. In a corner, rain was falling on a tree. Adelaide had brought it home from the day-care center the day before she died.

After Denise left Allen and Jennifer went for a long walk to talk things over. "If we go and meet this child and we don't like her, what do we do then? Will she know we came to look her over? What are we doing, Allen? Do we know?"

"I thought we were going to like any child they gave us. That's what we said we'd do."

"I meant it. As long as the child isn't mean. I don't want someone who's mean. Or mentally handicapped. I couldn't handle that. Well, I couldn't."

"We're going to see what happens. I'm willing to take a chance on that, on anything. I want to fill our lives with life again, Jennifer. Remember when Mother said we should get some dogs. Can you imagine us filling this hole with dogs? Not that I don't like dogs. Christ." They had stopped on a corner by a building project, a huge house on a small corner lot. "Look at that," he continued. "Maybe we'll be like that. They didn't know what they were doing. They just started building and now they have this monstrosity on their hands. We could be like that. We could end up with some terrible problem we can't handle. But I have one now. Our house is so empty and quiet. We've gotten quiet. We have to fight back if we're going to live."

She was beginning to cry and he reached out and pulled her into his arms.

"We can't replace her," Jennifer said.

"We aren't trying to. We're going back into life. Dickie's a child psychiatrist, for God's sake. You used to be a teacher. I used to barrel race. Do you think there's a reasonably healthy child on the planet we can't save?"

"We'll find out." She held on to her husband for dear life, right out on the street at six o'clock in the afternoon. For the first time in months she felt desire, real desire, and she was going home and do something about it.

At three that morning she woke and went into the kitchen and took the drawing off the refrigerator and put it in her desk.

"So what did you do then?" Gabriela was asking. She and her friend Annie were sitting out in the yard talking. It was late in the day and they were trying to find something to do until supper. There wasn't much to do, but you could always sit on the boards by the fence and talk about things.

"I kicked him in the balls and ran for it. What do you think I did? I've told you about this before. Then he gets up and starts chasing me but he can't catch me. I used to be so fast I could outrun everyone. I'll probably get all soft and fat living with a bunch of girls. There's nobody in this place who could whip me."

"I know there's not, but Sister Felicia might hit you if you don't do your homework. She might not have been kidding about that. I heard she beat the shit out of some girls."

"I never saw her do that."

"Well, how long have you been here?"

"Two months before you came. I can't remember what month it was. I was glad to get here, I can tell you that. I was about worn out by the time they took me out of Doris's place. She was on the scam. She had six kids and she didn't give any of us a thing. I didn't have a pair of shoes that fit."

"Don't talk about it. I don't like to think they were mean to you."

"It was okay. I'm glad it happened or I wouldn't have met you." Annie put her hand on Gabriela's black curls and patted them down. Gabriela was the best kid she had ever had for a roommate and gave her half her food. Anything with sugar in it, Gabriela saved half of it for her. "My mother was fat," she added. "I guess I'll have to get fat too."

"You might not." Gabriela put her hand on top of Annie's hand and left it there. "You look great, Annie. You're the strongest-looking girl I've ever seen."

"Let's go in." Annie squeezed the small hand. "Let's go see what they have for dinner."

On Monday Jennifer and Allen Williams boarded a plane and flew to San Diego. They rented a car and drove to Potrero and found the orphanage. It was a stucco and brick building that had been a school. It sat on a flat brown patch of land that turned to mud when it rained and a dust bowl when it was dry. The only redeeming architectural feature of the place was the covered walkway that led from the main building to the wooden dormitory.

Jennifer was wearing a batik skirt and a soft pink blouse. She had put on makeup very carefully. "We shouldn't look sad," she said to Allen. "We have to try not to look sad."

"We are sad," he answered. "But maybe we won't always be." It was one of the things he had begun saying. He didn't believe it yet but he kept saying it as though to trick it into being so. In many ways Allen was more shaken than his wife by what had happened. He was the one who had dropped their child off at the day-care center. He had identified the body. He didn't care what happened now. If Jennifer wanted a child, he had made up his mind to follow her and do what she wanted. At least she had an idea. Allen had run out of ideas. The one thing he believed was that he would sleep again. He no longer believed in God but he believed in the future more than Jennifer did. She had an idea and she was willing to follow wherever it led, but he believed that things would get better.

"When did you decide to adopt?" Sister Maria Rebecca had served them tea and crackers. She was seated behind her desk. They sat before her on the matching rattan chairs.

"A month ago. At least a month. We called Denise, the woman you talked to, about two weeks ago. We're not chasing some whimsical idea. Anyone in Oklahoma City will tell you who we are. Father Matthew sent you a letter. If you want to read it." Jennifer got the letter from her purse. "We want to be of use to a child. That's it. That's the only thing we know. If you can help us."

"I'm an attorney," Allen put in. "I was taking depositions at the Social Security Administration. That's why our daughter was there. It was only for that week, as Jennifer had to be gone. Jennifer doesn't need to work. She could stay home with the child. We would never leave another child at a day-care center, or anywhere. We aren't unlucky people. We think this is a good decision, a wise, planned idea." He sat up straighter, took a breath. It was very hot in the room. Sister Maria Rebecca had not moved a muscle. She didn't look as if she believed anything they were saying. He took a deep breath, he went on. "I have five brothers. I know all about children. We would have had more children than Adelaide but they never came. We aren't trying to replace our child."

"Denise said there was a little girl named Gabriela," Jennifer added. "She said she was healthy. I don't care about anything else but I guess I hope she will be healthy. We have cold winters but our house is warm. We're healthy people."

"I must make sure you totally understand this situation. Gabriela has had a bad time. Frankly, we don't know much about her life before she came to us and she won't talk about it. She is, how shall I say it, sometimes fierce. She bit the last two people who tried to keep her. She tears things up."

"She can tear things up where we live," Jennifer said. "We don't give a damn. Excuse me, Sister. We have a swimming pool.

Allen makes a hundred thousand dollars a year. We don't drink. We have a good life. Does she speak English?"

"As well as Spanish. She likes to talk. I told her some people from Oklahoma were coming to meet her. That she might want to go stay with you if she liked you. She said she wanted to see your car." The sister smiled. Allen began to laugh.

"We have a red one that we rented. And we have two at home."

"I'll get her," Sister Maria Rebecca said. "Wait here."

In a few minutes she returned, bringing Gabriela by the hand. Gabriela was wearing her blue uniform and the long brown cape trailing behind her on the dusty floors. She stood in the doorway and waited, her hair a messy crown above the turned-up collar of the dress.

Jennifer moved across the room and knelt beside her. "We need a little girl to come and live with us," she said. "Will you try us out? Will you try to get to know us?"

"Well, I can sing for you," Gabriela said. "I know a bunch of songs."

"I play the piano and the guitar." Allen moved across the room toward them. "I love music. I love to sing."

"Okay. Here's the song." Gabriela spread the cape back with her elbows. She raised her head and began to sing:

> Turkey in the oven. Tinsel on the tree.
> Something in the chimney. Sounds like a squirrel to me.
> Oh, there is a time of year that I love the best.
> Christmas is the name of it. Time of Jesus' birth.

"I can sing it better than that if I want to. We learned that at Wallace's house. They had bad food there. Do you have good food where you live?" She pulled her arms back under the cape and turned her eyes on Allen.

"We sure do. If you don't like what we have we'll go to the store and buy something else. We heard you were interested in cars. We have a new blue car and an old black car."

Gabriela took a long deep breath that was almost a sigh. Then she walked across the room and stood by Sister Maria Rebecca's desk. "Could we take Annie with us?" she asked. "Annie wants to go to a house."

"Who is Annie?" Jennifer asked, but Sister Maria Rebecca was shaking her head.

"She's this girl who sleeps by me. She's my friend. You want to see her?"

"Sure we do," Allen said. He hadn't asserted himself in so long he was surprised by the sound of his own voice.

"Okay," Gabriela said and turned and left the room. Sister Maria Rebecca stood up. She had decided to let chance have its way. Before she became a nun she had been a large, homely girl from Lincoln, Nebraska. Sometimes she knew how to step back and let things go.

"They form attachments," she said. "Annie is a lazy girl. She doesn't work at school. She's a big lazy girl and she fights. But not mean. I don't think she's mean." She sat back down. Allen and Jennifer looked at each other and began to laugh. They didn't want to laugh. They were trying not to laugh. Allen gave in to it but Jennifer resisted. She felt like she was on a roller coaster ride. She had set out to do a Christian act and now she was sitting in a rattan chair getting ready to be introduced to a big lazy girl who fights.

"We believe Annie's father was Australian," Sister Maria Rebecca went on. "A merchant marine. The agency has tried to find him but to no avail. Her mother died in an automobile accident in San Diego and the relatives couldn't take her. She's been in several foster homes. Would you want two girls? It might be easier in many ways if you could afford it."

"We knew when we came down here we were going to a world we couldn't imagine," Allen said. "It is amazing, Sister. The work you do. How do you carry all their stories in your head?"

"I don't think of it. I'm only the instrument. I get up in the morning and try to do my work. We are always short of money, of course. Every month is a struggle. Then, sometimes, a miracle happens. It would help if you took two girls. That would leave room for two more. This is a paradise compared to many of the places they are living."

"I hadn't thought of two." Jennifer looked worried. "But we have room for two. Gabriela is a precious child, Sister. She's more than I could have imagined. She's so pretty."

"She's a riot," Allen added. "We could get her in a children's theater. Oklahoma City is big on theater. There are all sorts of classes and groups. I can't believe she just started singing. And what's with the long brown cape?"

"She's always dressing up in something," Sister Maria Rebecca said. "She ties things around her waist."

Gabriela returned with Annie. They had washed her face and combed part of her hair. She was a big girl with wide shoulders, just at the most awkward age for girls. Gabriela brought her into the room and stood beside her holding her hand. "Here she is. What do you think?"

"I think we should all go for a drive in the car," Allen said. "If that's all right with Sister. We could go into Potrero and get some dinner. Would you trust these young women with us, Sister? I'm hungry after all this traveling."

"Have them back by nine." Sister Maria Rebecca began to hope. This had the makings of a minor miracle. She was hungry too. For the stew she knew the kitchen was making and for something good to come of something. Why shouldn't these four forlorn human beings come together, she asked God. I will pray on this and you will be merciful, I am sure.

Annie and Gabriela climbed into the backseat of the rented car. They rolled the windows up and down. They pulled up the floor mats and looked underneath them. They moved the ashtray up and down.

"Where would you like to go?" Allen asked as he drove back out onto the street. "What would you like to do?"

"Annie likes food," Gabriela said. "If we go get some food Annie will eat it."

"Shut up," Annie said. "Why'd you say that?"

"What kind of food do you like?" Jennifer asked. "There's a whole strip of restaurants in Potrero. We'll drive by them and let you pick one out."

"Not Tex-Mex," Annie said. "I'd like something different for a change."

"We might find someplace that has music," Allen suggested. "Do you like music too, Annie?"

"Do I like it? Fucking-A I like it. Me and Gabriela sing all the time. That's how we stand this place. This one place I lived, this guy had so many CDs you couldn't find a place to sit. He worked in a record store before he lost his job. That's where I learned all the songs. I taught a bunch of them to Gabriela, didn't I?"

"Let's just go get some hamburgers before we starve to death," Gabriela said. "We can save the music for later. I'd rather just get a hamburger and some French fries and not mess around."

"You want to put on your seat belts." Jennifer turned around and faced them. "I really think you ought to put them on. Do you know how?"

"Oh, sure, we'll take care of that." Annie reached over and strapped Gabriela in. She smelled of mildew, as if her hair had not been washed in weeks. Jennifer was having to work to even like the child but she wanted to shampoo her hair and she had forgotten the headache she had had for months. There seemed to be so much going on that she felt like she might have to run to catch up with it.

"Go to McDonald's, Allen," she said. "Let's eat and then we'll find a mall. I might get my hair done at a beauty parlor if they have one. Anyone else want to do that?"

An hour later they were eating hamburgers. Then they were in a mall beauty parlor taking turns getting their hair shampooed. Annie panicked while the shampoo was on and had to be held down to get it rinsed. Only the promise of cookies kept her still while she was combed out and dried.

Then they were in a shoe store buying shoes. Gabriela bought some red patent leather shoes with straps and Annie bought the most expensive running shoes in the store. No one argued with either of them. The girls picked out shoes and Allen paid for them and they wore them out of the store.

On the way back to the orphanage the girls fell asleep in the car. Annie was on the bottom, with Gabriela curled on top of her. "What will we do?" Jennifer whispered. "Do we just take them home and say we'll see you in the morning?"

"What do you want to do?"

"I want Gabriela to come home with us."

"And Annie?"

"I don't know. I don't know if I'm up to it. She's almost a teenager."

"We don't have to decide tonight."

"Where is Denise when we need her? We should have brought her with us."

"I want Annie." He said it very quietly. "She tugs at my heart. And Gabriela needs her. They're a pair. How could we split them up?"

"Be quiet. They might hear you." Jennifer undid her seat belt and turned around on the seat to look at the girls. They were so sound asleep they seemed to be dead. Annie's right hand was on one of her new shoes. Her left hand was around Gabriela's shoulder.

They were late getting home to the orphanage. Sister Maria Rebecca was waiting for them at the door. "How did it go?" she asked, taking the sleepy girls into the foyer. "Did you get along all right?"

"We'll come back tomorrow," Allen said. "As soon as we have breakfast."

"Are you going to take us to your house?" Gabriela asked. "You think we're the girls you want or not?"

"Oh, darling girl." Jennifer went to her and hugged her. Then she hugged Annie. "Tomorrow we'll talk about it and see if you want to come."

"So what's the deal?" Annie asked but the sister handed them to a younger nun who took them off down the hall.

"Think it over," Sister Maria Rebecca said. "Come back to-morrow while they're in their classes. We will talk about it then."

"Could we have them both?"

"Annie's far behind in school. Very far behind. Think it over and we'll talk tomorrow. God speed."

*   *   *

"They won't take us anywhere," Annie was saying. "I've seen that look before. Once some people kept me a couple of weeks. They looked like that the whole time."

"What'd you do?"

"I just ate everything I could get my hands on and watched their television set. He beat her up the day before they took me back. I was glad to leave. He'd be beating on me next."

"I think they want us to go with them. They've got a horse and a trampoline and a piano. I was being as nice to them as I could be."

"I was too. I couldn't help it when they got that shampoo on my face. That was about to kill me."

"You want to sleep over here with me?"

"Sure. Why not. I like this cover you got out of the box. This is warm as a sweater."

"Pull it up around your neck. Doesn't it smell good? I think it smells like some kind of flower."

"Fucking-A. Well, go to sleep. At least we got some shoes."

Jennifer and Allen got into the rented car and drove very slowly back to town. "I think we ought to take them both," Allen said. "We didn't come all the way down here to end up feeling guilty and harming some eleven-year-old girl. The little one doesn't want to go without her."

"She's a dream, isn't she? All that life and spirit after God knows what kind of life. Picking out those red dancing shoes. I couldn't believe that was what she wanted."

"Annie walked around the store reading the price tags. She got the most expensive shoes in the store. Did you see her looking at the insoles? She was inspecting them like they were diamond bracelets. She isn't dumb, Jennifer. She's as bright as she can be. Think where she might end up."

"I don't know, Allen. She's so coarse, so crude."

"She's alive, Jennifer." Allen speeded up. "She's a living, breathing child. I could teach her to ride. You could teach her to read. We'll catch her up. Or she won't catch up and I'll teach her to rodeo. You know why I am insisting on this, besides not hurting them? Because the whole time we were in that mall I didn't think about Adelaide. I think that's the first time since the bombing that I've been free of pain. All I could see was their pain. How hard they were trying to please you. She was scared to death in that beauty parlor. She might never have seen one, much less been in one."

"That bothered me when she picked out those expensive shoes. I saw her reading all the tags."

"Think of how she's been cheated all her life. She was trying to make sure she got something back for the night. Hell, I liked that about her more than anything either of them did. They're survivors, both of them. We could do it, Jennifer. We can take them out of here and make a life for them. I feel it in every bone in my body."

"This was my idea," she said, sliding back into the seat. She had not seen Allen acting powerful in a long time. It took her by surprise. "And now you've taken it over. Okay. Let's go over there in the morning and throw ourselves into this. Let's get ready for the worst. They'll bite us or tear something up."

"They won't bite us." Allen pulled her over close to him and held her there. "They will eat us out of house and home or teach us to live on junk food. Actually I like junk food, Jennifer. Did I ever tell you that? Have you forgotten that?'"

"Have them take everything out of Adelaide's room," Jennifer told her mother on the phone that night. "Everything. Take every single thing and give it away. Have someone come in and paint. Yellow and white. Yellow. Bright yellow. Then order some twin beds. Can you do that in five days? Call Dan Mahew. He'll get it painted. One is seven and the other one is almost twelve. Don't worry about it. We'll tell you when we get home. And some bicycles if you have time. And food. Get a lot of food. I don't care. Good food. Things that taste good. Don't ask me a lot of questions, Mother. Just do the best you can and call me back tomorrow night. I have to go. We're taking them to San Diego to buy some clothes to wear home on the plane.

". . . I don't care. I don't know. It doesn't matter. Don't worry about it. If they can't finish painting don't let them start. Just clean it up. We'll be there in a few days. As soon as we get the paperwork in order. This is what we're doing, Momma. And Allen said if you can, call Mr. Harrod to tune the piano. Leave him a key.

". . . A key. A key to the door. . . . Of course he can be trusted with it. He lives a block down the street. Don't talk about money. Money doesn't matter. It has nothing to do with this. And get ready to like them, Momma. Get down on your knees and pray for understanding. Because you might need it. I'm not telling you another thing. You'll have to wait and see."

We all have to wait and see, she decided, when she hung up the phone. That's all anyone is ever doing anyway, only most of the time we don't know it.

A Wedding by the Sea

THE WEDDING HAD been planned for June. Then for August. Now it was the tenth of September and at last Nieman Gluuk and Stella Light had set a date they wouldn't break.

"We are mailing the invitations today," Stella told Nora Jane. They were having tea on the patio of the Harwoods' house on the beach. It was Friday morning. Stella was missing a faculty meeting about grants for the graduate students, but the dean had let her go. No one was expecting much of Stella or Nieman this year. The world will always welcome lovers. This is especially true on the Berkeley campus, where many people have thought themselves almost out of the emotional field. "We have set a deadline. Every invitation in the mail before we sleep. Are you sure you want to have it here? This close to the baby coming?"

The women were sitting on wicker chairs with a small table between them. The table held cheese and crackers and wild red strawberries and small almond wafers Stella had brought for a gift. "I told the department head I had to have a week and he said, Take two weeks." Stella shook her head. "I think we'll just go to the Baja and lie in the sun and read. I have never imagined myself being married. It seems like such an odd, old rite of passage. Are you sure you want to have it here?"

"Freddy Harwood would die if he couldn't have this wedding here. He is fantastically excited about it. So are the girls. Did you bring a list?"

Stella fished it out of her jacket pocket and handed it over. "It's seventy names. This one is my cousin in Oklahoma City. The one who lost a child in the bombing. They have two foster children they're trying to adopt. So I think they will bring them. Two little girls they found in a Catholic home down on the border. One's eleven and the other's seven. My mother's been very involved in it. She specializes in children with learning disorders. They had to round up all sorts of counseling. They were kids no one else wanted to adopt. Anyway, they are coming to the wedding."

"Maybe they should be bridesmaids. Tammili and Lydia would love some help." Nora Jane stretched her legs out in front of her. She was eight months pregnant. Sometimes she forgot about it for hours, then the baby would start moving and remind her.

"I should have thought of that. Of course they can be in the wedding. But how will we get them dresses? Don't the dresses all have to match?"

"That's easy. Bridesmaids' dresses are big business. I'll have a shop here send them things or they can send measurements and we'll have dresses waiting for them. Where are they going to stay?"

"I made reservations at the Intercontinental."

"Let your cousin's family stay with us. The guest house is just sitting there. Four little bridesmaids. This is starting to sound like a wedding."

"I'll call Jennifer tonight. Momma said they were nice little girls. She said it's working out a lot better than anyone thought it would. It's been a godsend to me. It kept Momma off my back while Nieman and I decided what to do."

That was Friday morning. By Monday afternoon a bridal shop in San Francisco and one in Oklahoma City were deep in consultation on the subject of four pink bridesmaids' dresses that must be ready by October the sixteenth. The four little girls had been introduced on a conference call and Nora Jane Harwood and Jennifer Williams had gone past discussing dresses and hats and shoes and flowers and were into the real stuff. "You just went down there and got them?" Nora Jane asked. It was the fourth time they had talked.

"We had to live. When I saw them, my heart almost burst. They aren't a thing alike. Annie looks like she belongs in Minnesota. We still haven't figured out how she ended up in Potrero. But Gabriela is a little Mexican Madonna. Her ambition is to be a singer and get rich. She is very interested in getting rich."

"Can you adopt them?"

"We don't know yet. It's pretty certain we can have Annie but there aren't any papers on Gabriela. We're just living from day to day. I think if anyone tried to take them Allen would run away to Canada with them. Actually, the people here seem to think it will be all right. We're trying not to worry about it."

"This wedding is going to be amazing. It keeps growing. Freddy and Nieman found a string quartet and it's been in the papers twice. 'The famous iconoclastic bachelor Nieman Gluuk,' that's what they're calling Nieman."

"What are they calling Stella?"

"'Brilliant, reclusive scientist' was in the *Chronicle.* Freddy's teasing them to death about it."

"We will be there," Jennifer said. "I don't think either of them have ever been to a big wedding."

It was several weeks before eleven-year-old Annie started worrying about going to California to the wedding. Once she started, the worry fed upon itself. She began lying on her bed in the afternoon pretending to be asleep. Also, she started eating everything in sight.

"Don't you want to jump on the trampoline?" seven-year-old Gabriela asked her. "Don't you want to do anything?" She had known something was wrong with Annie for several days but this was the first time she had felt like doing anything about it. It was nice living in Oklahoma City, but Gabriela was getting worn out with all the things she had to do to keep it together.

Keeping Jennifer happy, letting Allen teach her to play the piano, trying to learn the arithmetic at school, talking Annie into taking her pills. The doctor had given Annie some pills that were supposed to keep her from getting mad at people, but she was afraid they would poison her and Gabriela had to help talk her into swallowing them. Sometimes Annie was afraid she would choke to death swallowing them and sometimes she just thought they might be poison. Gabriela would get on one side of Annie and Jennifer would get on the other side and Gabriela would say, "Would I let you get poisoned? Jennifer got them at a drugstore, Annie. She knows the guy who sold them to her. You swallow food all the time and it doesn't choke you, does it? It would take a lot of pills to make a French fry." Then Gabriela would take a piece of cereal or bread and demonstrate swallowing it and in the end they would usually get Annie to take the pill.

"You better let us keep them in our room," Gabriela advised Jennifer and Allen. "That way she'll know nobody's trying to slip her something."

"I'll take her to the drugstore to get the prescription filled," Allen suggested.

"Yeah, well, I knew a guy who worked in a place where they made pills." Annie was backed into a corner of the living room sofa. They were all around her. "He said they threw in rat shit when they got in a bad mood. He said you wouldn't believe what all was in pills you buy at the store."

Allen and Jennifer looked at each other. Both of them sort of half believed it. It was not the first revelation these girls from the lost half-world of the Mexican border had brought them.

Allen sat down on the floor. "Well, look at it like this," he began. "We have a system of trust in our culture. We all eat and drink things all day long that other people have handled and we have to believe that our inspectors, the people who go into factories where pills are made, are doing a good job of seeing that the things they sell us are clean and made out of the right things, not out of rat feces. Most of the people who make things for us do a good job of it, just like we would if we worked there.

I'll find out where the pills come from, Annie. I'll find out where the factory is and I'll call them and see if they're doing a good job before you take any more of them."

"That's right," Gabriela added. "I guess you got to think of it as getting lucky. If your luck's good, you don't get poisoned or raped or anything. If your luck runs out, you're fucked." She looked at Jennifer. She was trying not to say *fuck* around Jennifer. Jennifer smiled and went to her and touched her shoulder.

"It's okay," she said. "Say anything you want to say. So, Annie, what should we do? Should we trust the doctor and this druggist and take these pills or not? I don't want you to be scared every day when you have to take them."

"She'll take them." Gabriela went to her friend. "You're going to take them, aren't you? Look at me, Annie. Say something about it."

"I'm taking her to the drugstore to see where they come from," Allen said. "We'll find out where they're made. Maybe we can call the company and check on them."

"Okay. Give it here." They handed Annie a pill and watched as she swallowed it.

"Okay," Gabriela said. "Now let's talk some more about what we're going to get for our birthdays."

The next afternoon Allen took Annie to the drugstore and they talked to the druggist about where the pills were made and looked them up in the *PDR* and the druggist let Annie watch him put them in the bottle.

"You can keep them in your room," Allen said. "In a safe place. Every morning when you take one you can write it down in a notebook." They found the stationery department and picked out a pink notebook with a pencil attached. When they got home Annie put the pills and the notebook on a shelf in her closet.

"Tell us that again," she asked Allen that night. "That part about everybody trusts everybody else not to poison them."

*   *   *

"You think it's wise to let her keep them in her room?" Jennifer asked later.

"She needs to learn to write down dates. It will serve several purposes. I don't want her taking that stuff for long, Jennifer. The warnings in the *PDR* are pretty scary. It's just a form of Dexedrine. Why did Doctor Cole think she needed it?"

"Just to calm her down until we can get her settled in school. He says she's plenty bright. He just wants to make sure she doesn't get further behind and get the idea that she's dumb. Thank God for the sisters. She's going to stay in the fifth grade no matter what we have to do."

"She liked the notebook. I don't think she's had much of her own. Did you see the way she arranged her things in the room? She touches my heart, Jennifer. I can't believe how much I am attached to her already."

"Gabriela wants a savings account. She asked me to take her to my bank. Where did she find out about banks?"

"I'd be afraid to ask." They shook their heads in disbelief at what they had brought into their lives. Neither of them said Adelaide and neither of them had to. She was there, alive in their hearts and in every moment. World without end, amen.

On top of everything else she had to do, when Annie started acting funny about going to the wedding, Gabriela decided it was up to her to fix it. "I'll talk to her," she told Jennifer. "I can always get her to say what's wrong with her."

"How do you do it?" Jennifer asked.

"I just keep after her until she tells me. She's never afraid of anything except stuff that isn't true. She gets ideas in her head. She may be worrying about the airplane. She didn't like flying here too much but we didn't want to tell you."

That afternoon after school Gabriela cornered Annie in their room while she was changing clothes and started in on her. "Are you afraid of going on the airplane?" she asked. "You think it's going to crash or something?"

"I think they won't bring us back. I think they'll leave us there. They'll take us back to the home."

"No they won't. Jennifer says we're the reason she and Allen are alive."

"It's costing too much money. They have to pay the doctor and they have to buy me those pills. They cost twenty-four dollars. When I went to the drugstore with Allen to meet that guy that bottles them up I saw the bill. Twenty-four dollars for that little bottle that wasn't even full. They have to buy us all that food. They're going to get tired of that. They'll send us back."

Gabriela moved over and began to stroke Annie's hair. "They don't want to get rid of us. Would they buy us all these clothes if they weren't going to keep us? Not to mention that saddle Allen got you. Listen, you were so cute in that play last week. I bet Allen and Jennifer think you're the cutest girl they could ever get in the world. Come on, don't hide your face." Annie was starting to smile, thinking about the applause at her school play. Gabriela pressed her advantage. "If you'll stop worrying about going on the plane, I'll tell you what we'll do."

"What?"

"We won't be taking any chances. Wait a minute." Gabriela walked over to a painted chest at the foot of her bed and opened it and took out the brown cape. She arranged the cowl. "All right. Here's what we'll do. We will take this cape with us. This cape has been very lucky for us. The day we got it Sister Maria Rebecca told me about Allen and Jennifer coming to meet me. And it made you remember your lines last week when I made you sleep with it, didn't it? Admit it. Say something, Annie."

"Where do you think it came from?"

"I think some old monk had it in Nevada or somewhere, or else it's real old. Lucky stuff doesn't have to come from somewhere. You know when something's lucky for you."

"Okay. It's lucky for us."

"Then we'll take it to California to keep our luck going. Those girls we talked to on the phone are waiting for us. They're rich as they can be. They're going to make their dad take us to an amusement park. This is going to be a vacation, Annie. I never went on a vacation in my life. I want to go on one."

"All right," Annie said. "I'll go to this wedding. If I get to carry the cape."

"You can carry it. But if you lose it, I'll kick your butt. Do you get that?"

"I'd like to see you try." Annie stood up and grabbed her smaller friend around the waist and wrestled her to the bed. They fought for a minute, then they started laughing. The cape had gotten tangled around their legs. Besides, it was hard to fight without making any noise and it scared Jennifer to death if they punched each other. They had almost given up having fights, which was a shame because they were beautifully matched, despite the difference in their sizes. Annie was a wrestler, who liked to get holds on people and then sit on them or twist their arms. Gabriela was a stomach puncher and a shin kicker and a biter. She was also a good spitter and had won several battles at the home by spitting on people at crucial points in a fight.

The bridal shop in San Francisco mailed the dresses to the bridal shop in Oklahoma City. They were dresses by Helen Morley, who had also designed the dress Stella was going to wear. Stella's dress was elegant and simple, thick white silk with embroidery down the back and capped sleeves and a high neck.

The dresses for the girls were made of pale pink lace over satin slips. There were tiers of lace ten inches wide going down to the ankles and high-waisted bodices and full soft sleeves. When the owner of the shop in Oklahoma City pulled the first dress from the box a sigh went around the room. "Well," she said. "California always has to outdo everybody."

"They have all those Asian ideas," a saleslady comforted her. "Plus Hollywood."

"Yeah," said a third. "What do you expect?" Then the ladies recovered from their moment of jealousy and one ran off to comb the neighborhood for shoes. Another ran out to a rival store for gloves. A third began to work on the veils, which had been crushed in the mail.

At five that afternoon Jennifer and Annie and Gabriela arrived at the store and were ushered into a huge dressing room with golden chairs and a golden sofa. The girls took off their school clothes and were dressed in the pink lace costumes.

"I wasn't expecting this," Annie said. "How much does this dress cost?"

"This is for the Queen of Sheba," Gabriela agreed. "How are we going to wear this on a sandy beach?"

"Shit," Annie added, turning to see the back in the three-way mirror. "We look like a bunch of hibiscus flowers by the well."

"Fucking merde." Gabriela went to stand by her taller friend in the mirror. Even then the dresses looked perfect.

"Fucking-A," Annie agreed.

"Well, let's try on the gloves and shoes," the owner said. "We sent Roberta all over town to find shoes. We think white patent sandals since it's by the water."

The saleslady named Roberta began to open the shoeboxes that were stacked in the corner. "Every size they could possibly wear," she said proudly. "I looked all over town. We aren't going to be outdone by anyone in California. They will arrive with everything they need." Except mouthwash, she was thinking, and then chastised herself for being mean. Everyone in Oklahoma City knew the Williamses' story.

Annie sat down on the sofa and allowed Roberta to try the shoes on one by one. "You might consider shaving her legs," Roberta said. "I started shaving mine in the sixth grade."

Annie bent over and looked at the elegant little sandals on her feet. She examined the small, light-colored hairs showing along her bones. She pursed her lips.

"Her legs are perfect," Jennifer was saying. "She doesn't need to shave her legs."

"She's right," Annie muttered. "That looks like shit. I know how to shave it off. I seen a girl in the home doing it. You get me a razor and a bar of soap and I'll take care of that."

"Do you like the shoes? Is that pair comfortable? Get up and walk around in them."

Annie got up from the couch and began to parade around in front of the mirrors. What would it be like, being in a wedding? The priest would be fixing the wine. The altar boys would be swinging incense. Everyone would be looking at her. She stood very still, lost in thought. Gabriela moved across the room and took her arm. "Don't start getting moody," she said in a whisper. "Ask them if we're just going to wear these dresses, or if we're going to get to keep them."

"I need the shoes with the heels on them," she said in a louder voice to Jennifer. "If I wear those little ones I'll look like a midget."

It was seven that night when Jennifer and the girls got home from the store. They had gloves and hats and shoes in an assortment of sacks and boxes. The dresses had been left to be altered and hemmed. "So now do you think they would get rid of you?" Gabriela asked Annie, when they were alone in their room getting ready for bed. "After they got you a dress that cost about two hundred dollars and all that other stuff that matches it?"

"I've got to get me a razor," Annie answered. "I've got to shave these fucking hairs off my legs."

It stormed in the night. A huge thunderstorm that roared in about twelve o'clock and woke up the town. Jennifer and Allen lay in bed listening to the hail hit the roof. Then they went into the kitchen and got out food. They got out potato chips and sliced chicken and mayonnaise and lettuce and tomatoes and chocolate chip cookies and Gatorade. Since the girls had been there they had completely altered their diet and gone back to eating things that tasted good. "Something's bothering Annie," Jennifer said. "She's worrying about something and I don't know how to ask her what it is. I don't know if I should wait for Doctor Cole to find out or ask her. I don't know how far to pry into her mind. What would it be like, to be here with us, to think you were on probation, whether you were or not? What else can we do?"

"She's been knocked around from pillar to post all her life. How could she keep from worrying? If she's breathing, we're ahead. But I don't like her taking Ritalin, Jenny. That's a class four drug. Ever since we went through that business with going

to the drugstore I've been reading up on it. I don't think they
ought to be giving her drugs for anything, even to make her do
better in school."

"Did you ask your brother?"

"He agrees it isn't the best idea but Cole is the only child
psychiatrist he could find us on short notice. He said it would
be all right to let her take it for a month or so until he can find
another doctor."

"It seems to help."

"Drugs are for sick people. She's not sick. I thought we
weren't going to care if they didn't act like normal children. I
thought they were going to tear things up. I was hoping they'd
break some of that bric-a-brac of Mother's in the living room. I
hate that bric-a-brac. I was looking forward to seeing it in piles
on the floor." Allen brandished his chicken sandwich. He added
more mayonnaise and took a bite.

"I didn't know you hated the bric-a-brac. I hate it too. If you
hate it, let's go take it down. We have those boxes the encyclopedia came in. We'll take it down and put it in them."

"Okay. Let's do it." Allen ate one last bite of his sandwich,
grabbed a couple of potato chips, and led the way into the living
room. There, behind the sofa, was a wall of shelves holding the
remnants of his childhood, little cups and saucers and figurines
and glass statues and vases and bookends. "I used to be late for
baseball practice because I had to dust that stuff on Saturdays,"
he said. "Now I shall have my revenge." He began to take the
things from the shelves. Jennifer brought in a bag of newspapers they were saving to recycle and began to wrap the pieces
and put them in the encyclopedia boxes. They were almost finished removing every piece when Annie appeared in the door.

"That rain woke me up," she said. "You guys have the noisiest
weather I ever heard in my life."

"No mountains," Allen said. He went to her and put his arms
around her shoulders. He pulled her with him over to where
Jennifer was packing a kneeling Cupid into the last box. "Jennifer thinks you're worrying about something," he began. "So
we're worrying about you worrying. If you worry, we worry. We
know something's worrying you because we love you and we are

thinking about you. You want to tell us what's wrong, so we can worry about the right thing?"

"Why are you taking all this stuff down?" she asked.

"Because I'm sick of looking at it. We're going to put it in the garage. You don't want to talk about if something is worrying you?"

"I'm worried about going on that plane," she answered. "I don't see what holds it up."

"I'll show you what holds it up." Allen hugged her tighter, then let her go. "You have come to the right place with that question, Miss Annie. Did you know that I just so happen to know how to fly airplanes? Did you know that I also know how to fly a helicopter and flew them for three years in the United States Air Force?" He took the little girl to a table and opened a volume of the new encyclopedia which was still stacked in a corner waiting for him to get around to assembling the bookshelf that had come with it. He spread the encyclopedia down on a table and began to teach her the principles of aeronautics.

Two weeks went by. In Berkeley, everyone was busy getting ready for the wedding. The guest list kept expanding as friends Nieman and Stella hadn't heard from in months kept calling and asking where to send gifts. The gossip columns were full of the news. Also, the story of the girls from the home in Potrero had leaked out, adding to the public's interest.

In Salem, Oregon, Stella's mother was working out at a gym every afternoon hoping to lose weight so she wouldn't embarrass Stella by being fat. Stella's father was reading back issues of the *National Geographic* and pretending to ignore the whole thing. Nieman's mother was so mad she couldn't sleep. She had intended Nieman to marry a wealthy Jewish girl, preferably from New York City, and instead he had chosen this thirty-seven-year-old woman who didn't even wear eye makeup. "You can barely see her eyes," Bela Gluuk told her friends. "I doubt if she'll have her hair done for the ceremony. . . . No, of course not. No rabbi, not even a minister or a priest. Some woman judge, just to make me miserable, no doubt. What else has Nieman ever done?"

*   *   *

In Oklahoma City the day finally arrived to board the plane and fly to San Francisco. Annie clutched Allen's hand and climbed aboard the plane. She had the cape slung across her shoulder. "Why are you bringing that?" Jennifer asked. "They have blankets on the plane."

"It's something lucky we have," Gabriela explained. "I let her carry it for luck."

"Fine with me," Allen said. They found their seats on the DC-9. Allen and Jennifer were together with a seat in between them and Gabriela and Annie were across the aisle. "There is nothing to fear on this plane but the food," Allen whispered. "Don't lose that sack with the sandwiches and cookies."

"Allen," Jennifer said. "Keep your voice down. Don't let the stewardess hear you."

"At least I know it's my lucky day." Gabriela reached underneath the cape and took Annie's hand. "At least I lived long enough to have a vacation."

Annie squeezed the hand Gabriela had put in hers. She pushed the sack with the lunch around until she was holding it with both her feet. Allen and Jennifer tried not to laugh out loud. "She lived to go on a vacation," Jennifer whispered to him. "I have to start writing down the things she says."

Stella and Tammili met the Williams family at the airport. Lydia had not been able to come as she had a class on Friday afternoons. "So, how was your flight?" Tammili asked. She picked up Gabriela's backpack and carried it. Gabriela picked up Annie's pack and carried that. Annie carried the cape.

"I threw up," Annie said. "Allen told me why the plane stays up, but I stopped believing it when we were halfway here."

"I made her look out the window at the mountains. That's when it happened," Gabriela added. "I thought you had a twin sister. Where's the other girl?"

"She's at an acting class. We have to take a lot of classes so we'll have different interests. I don't do it anymore, but Lydia does everything they think up for her. So, how are things going in Oklahoma? You all getting along all right?"

"Except for storms," Gabriela answered. "Just when I thought

I was going to live someplace that doesn't have earthquakes, I get adopted by some people who live in Tornado Alley. That's what they call it there. It's okay, though. People wear a lot of colored clothes. Like all these old ladies have these pink outfits they wear to the mall. Do you all have malls around here?"

"We have Chinatown. Did you ever go to it when you lived out here?"

"Are you kidding? The nuns never took us anywhere. So, where's this wedding going to be anyway?"

"At our house. That's the best part. We don't have to ride in a car in our dresses and get them wrinkled. All we have to do is put them on and walk out to the patio." They had come to the baggage carousel and were standing beside the grown people, waiting for the luggage to come. Tammili moved nearer to Annie. She reached up and touched the cape. "That's weird," she said. "My sister and I had a cape like that. We lost it on a camping trip when Dad broke his arm. Where do you get those capes? Did you buy it in Oklahoma?"

"It's magic," Gabriela said. "It's got powers in it."

"So did the one we had. Listen, it stayed dry in this terrible rain. This synchilla blanket we had that's supposed to wick faster than anything you can buy, got wet, but that cape was still as dry as a bone."

"She thinks some monks in Nevada probably make them." Annie moved the cape until it was around both of her shoulders. "Gabriela thinks they make them and sell them to people to give them luck. We seen some monks in Potrero. A bunch of them came and stayed with us on their way to Belize. We had them there for a week but that was before Gabriela came. She never got to see them."

"I saw them. Where'd you think I saw monks if it wasn't for that bunch that came and stayed at the home? I got there the day they were leaving. I saw them all sleeping on the ground. This cape is just like the stuff they were wearing."

"We're Jewish," Tammili said. "We don't have any monks."

The bags arrived and a man in a uniform appeared and helped them carry the bags outside to a limousine.

"The limo's just for fun," Tammili said. "My dad thought

you'd like a limo, so we got you one. There're things to drink inside. Get in. See how you like it. Lydia and I adore limousines but we never get to get them because Dad usually says they're for movie people and Eurotrash."

The grown people got into the back and the girls got into the seats facing backward. Tammili was sitting next to Annie. She reached out and touched the cape again. She felt the softness of the weave caress her hand. "This is going to be the best wedding anyone ever had," she said. "I've been waiting all my life to be a bridesmaid. I don't care if it's bourgeois or not. I think it's the best."

"Well, I've never been in a wedding. I never even gave it much thought. I just hope I don't do something stupid."

"My parents' friends almost never get married. They just cohabit and have serial monogamy. So we are lucky this happened. You see, the groom is our godfather. He means a lot to us."

Annie and Tammili were deep in conversation, their heads turned to each other. Gabriela started getting jealous. "Did you take your pill this morning?" she put in, leaning toward them. "Where are they, Annie? Where did you put them?"

"I don't know," Annie answered. "I don't know where they are."

"Dad found this article in the *New York Times* about these people who have been getting orphaned babies from China," Tammili was saying. "We saved it to show you. Lydia and I are begging Mom and Dad to adopt some to go with the baby we're having. They said if we both made the honor roll for a year they'd think about it. Anyway, we saved the article for you. I mean, what you're doing is not that unusual. Well, this is San Francisco. That's the Golden Gate Bridge up there. We have to cross it to get to our house."

"She forgot her pills," Gabriela said to Jennifer. "Annie forgot her Ritalin."

"Good," Allen said. "She doesn't need any pills. I think that doctor's crazy to give pills to that child."

"She's taking Ritalin?" Stella asked. "I didn't think they still prescribed that to children. What are they giving her Ritalin for?"

"To get her adjusted to school," Jennifer answered. "Why? What do you know that we don't know?"

"It's just a very old-fashioned drug. Primitive, compared to the things we have now. How long has she been taking it?"

"A month. Almost a month. What's wrong with it, Stella?"

"I took a couple of them," Gabriela put in. "It didn't do anything to me but make me talk all the time. And, yeah, that day at school I did all that arithmetic so fast. I was wondering if that had anything to do with that."

"You took one?" All three of the adults leaned her way.

"I sure wasn't feeding them to Annie without knowing what she was taking. I seen, saw. I saw that happen with a girl in this place I stayed once. She took some pills this guy gave her and she ended up almost dying."

"You took a Ritalin?" Allen took both her hands in his. Stella began to breathe into a Zen koan.

"I cut one in two. I know about drugs. I used to help out at the home when kids got sick. Sister Elena Margarite said she might make a nurse of me."

"Where are they now?" Stella asked. "I'd like to see these pills."

"She left them at home. She wouldn't ever take them if I didn't remind her."

"It's all right," Jennifer said. "Forget about the Ritalin. When we get home we'll find another doctor."

"Was this my mother's doing?" Stella asked. "Is this some of Momma's old hippie connections she put you on to? Damn that woman. She and Dad are at a Ramada Inn waiting to hear from us. I've been praying for weeks they wouldn't come."

"Stella, how can you talk like that about your parents?"

"I'm an unnatural child. Nieman is too. That's why we're marrying each other. I finally met a man who isn't interested in meeting my family."

Annie had slid back into the seat, listening. These were the strangest adults she had ever encountered. All these days and weeks and they kept on acting just like they had the day she met them. As if life was funny, an adventure, something amazing to be watched and commented on. As if some light was in them that did not go out. She raised her eyes and they were smiling on her. Stella was looking at Gabriela.

"You got any crabs on this beach where your house is?" Gabriela asked Tammili. "I went to the beach a couple of times. These old birds were pecking for food in the sand and there were crabs underneath a log. I'd like to catch one in a bucket and get a good look at that if I could."

"We're almost there," Tammili told her. "We are almost to our house."

As soon as they arrived at the Harwoods' house, Stella excused herself and got into her car and drove to her office in the biochemistry building and started making phone calls and pulling things up on her computer. In an hour she had talked to child psychiatrists in New Orleans and New York City and Pittsburgh. She had researched recent antidepressants and had missed her appointment for a haircut. She stopped on her way home at a walk-in beauty parlor and let them even up the back and sides of her very short, severe haircut. She shook out the navy blue dress she was wearing to her rehearsal dinner and got into the shower still running the statistics on antidepressants through her head. Not good, she decided. Feeding Ritalin to a perfectly healthy child. She probably needs a shrink and Stella and Allen need to find out where she's been and what happened to her but I could figure that out if I had her alone for a week. Anxieties are like fingerprints but they are easily traced. What a fantastic cousin I have to think up something this crazy and wonderful and brave. I really like that girl. And the other one, the small one, is as pretty as a picture. What a lovely, ancient face. She looks like she's thirty years old inside. She took one of the pills! God, the human race. You can't see that underneath a microscope, Stella. There is nothing in RNA and DNA to account for our behavior, except the attachments we form are in the pattern, aren't they? Each of us has our receivers, what the old Jungians called the anima and animus, and someone comes along that fits the pattern and we meld. I am getting married in the morning to Nieman Gluuk. I am going to be his wife and make a home with him and be with him when we are old. Scary and wonderful, I guess.

She turned up the water in the shower and decided to stay there until the hot water ran out. The phone started ringing as soon as she got comfortable. She got out and answered it. "Stella," Nieman moaned on the telephone. "Where are you? I can't be alone waiting to get married. I'm coming over right this minute."

"Then I won't get dressed," she giggled. "Come on. Let's see what terror does to the parasympathetic nervous system."

"I'm in the car. I'll be there in ten minutes."

The living room of the Harwoods' house at the beach was an inspiration of the movers. They had moved all the musical instruments into one room while they waited for someone to arrive and give them orders. The Harwoods had left it that way. The room contained two baby grand pianos and a harpsichord and a harp. That was it. Except for a long thin table holding a Bose music system the size of a book.

"Fucking-A," Gabriela said when she saw it, forgetting her vow not to curse at the wedding.

"We had to get this house because my dad's bookstore keeps getting bombed," Tammili said. "My grandmother bought it for us. Don't worry about it being big. Most of it is wasted space. It was a wreck when we got it. We had to have the roof replaced and all the plumbing and the windows. The windows were so loose they rattled when it rained. So, there's the ocean. I guess that makes up for everything. And the guest house is nice. You'll like it there."

"What do you do with all these pianos?" Gabriela asked.

"We play them. Go ahead, try one. Come on. You can't hurt it. Momma's got a piano tuner who used to work for the symphony. He comes out every other month. Go on, play it. See how it sounds."

Gabriela walked over to the harpsichord and ran her fingers soundlessly across the keyboard. Nora Jane watched them from the doorway. "Would you like me to show you how?" she asked. "I have all these pianos because I was an orphan too. I have these pianos so I won't have to put up with feeling bad in case I ever do. I just come in here and start making noise. Come on, sit down by me." She sat down at one of the baby grand pianos. Gabriela sat beside her. Annie came and sat on the other side. She was still holding the cape over her shoulder like a shawl. Tammili stood behind her and laid her left hand very lightly on the cape. Nora Jane began to play show tunes, songs from Broadway musicals.

Tammili moved away from the piano. She began to dance. Gabriela got up and danced beside her. When Lydia came in the front door she found them dancing and joined them.

The wedding of Nieman Gluuk to Miss Stella Ardella Light began with children dancing.

The day of the wedding dawned bright and clear. By nine in the morning all four of the bridesmaids were dressed and wandering around the house getting in the way of the caterers. "Dahlias," Freddy Harwood declared. "The house is full of dahlias." Freddy was dressed in his morning suit and was videotaping everything in sight. He videotaped the bridesmaids in the music room and on the patio and in the kitchen. He videotaped the judge arriving with her twenty-six-year-old boyfriend. He videotaped Nieman and Stella getting out of Nieman's car and walking up the pathway to the back door. "He's scared to death," Freddy said into the microphone. "He's terrified. He can barely walk. He's making it. He's opening the door for her. It's nine-fifteen. Forty-five minutes until ground zero."

Nieman's mother arrived in a limousine. Stella's parents came in their Mazda van. The guests were crowding in. The driveway became packed with cars. The cars spread out across the lawn. The string quartet was playing Bach. Between nine-thirty and nine-forty-nine, a hundred and fifty people made their way up the front steps and filled the house. Someone handed bouquets to the bridesmaids. They formed a semicircle around the altar. The judge stepped into the middle. Nieman appeared. The quartet broke into a piece by Schubert. Stella joined her groom and the judge read a ceremony in which the bride and groom promised to do their best to take care of each other for as long as they lived and loved each other. Nieman kissed his bride. The audience heaved a sigh of relief and Champagne began to be passed on silver trays.

"That's it?" Annie said.

"I guess so," Lydia answered. "You want to get some petits fours and go play in my room?"

"We had a cape like this," she was saying later. She and Annie were lying on her bed with a plate of petits fours and wineglasses full of grape juice on her dresser. "We found a cape like this in this house we have that's in the hills. We took it on this hike with us and then we lost it."

"Your sister said the same thing. She said your dad broke his arm."

"We thought it was a lucky cape. Then we lost it."

"This one's lucky. As soon as Gabriela got it we got adopted. Just like that."

"I wish we could get another one. Do you know where to get them?"

"No. But I can't let you have this. It's Gabriela's. She just let me borrow it to fly on the airplane. So, is your dad going to take us to this amusement park?"

"He said he would if he could. If it opens before you have to leave tomorrow. I wish you could stay a few more days. There're a lot of things we could show you. We could take you on BART." Lydia lay facedown upon the cape, smelling the wonderful smell of wildflowers. "I think they make these out of some kind of flowers they grow somewhere. Like linen is made of flax. Where do you think they make them?"

"I think, Italy." Annie had no idea how she had decided to say Italy, but as soon as she said it she felt it was true. "I think they have this town in Italy and all they do is grow the flowers to make these capes."

*   *   *

"They think the cape is magic," Jennifer was saying. "They think they have a magic cape."

"What?" Nieman asked. "What are you talking about?"

"Like Michael Jordan wearing number twenty-three," Allen put in. "They believe in it, but they don't know we know they think it's magic. They just keep dropping hints."

They were on the side porch of the Harwoods' house. The wedding was winding down. The guests had nearly all gone home. The string quartet was in the kitchen talking to Freddy and Nora Jane. Jennifer and Allen Williams and the bride and groom were on the porch. It was the first time the Williamses had had a chance to be alone with the pair. Nieman had been commenting on how well the adopted girls had managed to fit into a scene they could not possibly have imagined. "Perhaps they saw it on a film," he had been saying. "I've written several times about how film teaches manners. Not just the obvious bad things, like violence, but also niceties, like how to hold your wedding bouquet. Do you think they were exposed to many films?"

"I don't know about that," Allen said. "But they have a cape they think is magic."

"They found the cape in a box of Salvation Army things a few days before we came to the home and met them. So they think it brought them luck. Technically, it's Gabriela's cape, but she lets Annie share it. She let Annie carry it on the plane. They pretended they wanted it for a blanket."

"I'm having a déjà vu," Stella said. She took Nieman's arm. She pressed herself into his side. "What is this all about?"

"I have it too," he said. "Just then. When Jennifer started talking about the cape. You have to understand," he said to Jennifer and Allen. "The first time we met we had this huge mutual déjà vu. Is this part of love, do you think? A harkening back to the mother–child relationship?"

"It's probably blood sugar," Stella said. "A magic cape. Well, that's a wonderful thing to believe you have. I found a really fine psychiatrist in Oklahoma City who will see her, Jennifer. I had to beg, but he'll see her once a week. Don't take her back to that man who gave her Ritalin. Promise you won't go back to him."

"Whatever you say, brilliant cousin," Jennifer answered. "It's unbelievable how much you learn to love a child, any child." She looked at Allen. "It's hard enough to suffer when you're old. Eleven years old should be a happy time and we want to make it one for her. If you found someone, we'll go and see him. I believe in psychiatry. I always have."

"I've thought of going into it," Stella said. "Sometimes I think I've taken molecular biology as far as it will go. Maybe I'll abandon the field to Nieman and get myself a new career." She closed her eyes, then opened them. "A dog runs across the street in front of your car. In a nanosecond the entire chemistry of the body changes. There are Buddhist monks who can regulate their heartbeat, control pain, choose when to die. There is so much to learn, so much to know." She turned to Nieman and kissed him on the lips. Jennifer clapped her hands, then kissed Allen long and passionately. It was the best kiss they had kissed in many months. A storm was brewing on the ocean. The negative ions were thick in the clean, sweet air.

"We'll come see you in August," Tammili was saying. "And you'll come here at Christmas when it's snowing where you live. We'll do that every year as long as we live and always be friends."

"We swear by the cape to be friends," Lydia added. The four little girls were sitting on the floor in their dresses. The cape was spread out between them. They were each holding part of it.

"Every time we see each other we'll get your dad to take videos of us," Gabriela put in. "In the meantime if he meets any movie people he can show them the videos and see if they want us to be in movies. Give them Jennifer and Allen's phone number if they do."